Tales from the
CANYONS of
the DAMNED

PRESENTED BY USA TODAY BESTSELLING AUTHOR
DANIEL ARTHUR SMITH

Tales from the Canyons of the Damned No. 25

First Edition

Special thanks to editor Jessica West

ISBN-13: 978-1946777638 ISBN-10: 1946777633

Cover By Daniel Arthur Smith

Horror Fiction from Holt Smith ltd
Agroland
Tower

For Susan, Tristan, & Oliver, as all things are.

Exodus Sol
P.K. Tyler

I

THIS IS THE VOICE OF THE PEOPLE. The only free transmission dedicated to serving all of Humanity. Our truth is your truth.

The familiar, eerie voice rang out through all of End's Reach Station, simultaneously transmitting throughout all the stations and public comms on Earth. It would reach into every home, every quarter, every office. The connectivity of information had been hacked. Again.

Castor sighed. It just meant more work.

An incoming probe has been detected from deep space. This probe will contain information those in power do not want the people to have. The viability of humanity's expansion effort is at stake. Will we travel to the stars or be kept in the dark ages as Earth around us dies? Over 11 billion people live on the planet and another 4 million are scattered on the colonies and stations off-world. Our options are limited. The people demand to know. What will happen to us next?

We promise you the truth, and we will find it. When the probe arrives, the data within will be hacked, and it will be shared. Do not ignore our warning. Without truth, hope is lost.

Static filled the airways, crackling and buzzing until it cut off suddenly, followed by the low drone of emergency status yellow.

Castor threw back the last of his drink. He dug out a coin and placed it on the table with a sharp tick. Only a few more months until he could transfer off this fucking station.

But at least it had gotten him off of Earth, the trash dump of the solar system.

End's Reach. The largest of the stations in the Sol System. They had thought it was the end of human expansion until the discovery of jump technology. Now, they sought habitable planets in the black.

The True Voice Movement had been making more and more announcements lately. They were more than just a nuisance, though. They sabotaged military vessels and stations. They'd even taken the Lunar Ring out of commission, slowing inner-solar travel for months until it had been repaired. They were dangerous.

Castor understood what they were trying to do, though no one would ever hear him say it out loud. He'd been raised on Earth, in the horrible leaving conditions. Polluted air, water, soil. Residential buildings over a hundred stories high and taking up entire city blocks. No one could afford to eat food or drink water. Hell, they could barely afford to breathe air.

But he didn't agree with the True Voice Movement's need to blow stuff up. He wasn't one to put too much thought in to things, but even he'd noticed how those attacks had always been followed by some corporation making a ton of money off it. Selling the ore to build new station walls or needing to replenish the oxygen supply. Or...or...or...

Always someone trying to make a buck off of others.

Exhausted and annoyed, he stood, smoothing down his shirt, and pulled his uniform jacket on. He buttoned the top and swiped his fingers over the two gold bars at his right collar.

Lieutenant. That only meant he had to deal with more shit from both sides.

End's Reach was the last station in the Sol System, located just inside Pluto's orbit. So, it was a little surprising that so many people could be crammed into one tiny place. It was a space station to nowhere. Sure, they had a jump ring, but there were no planets out there. Not that they knew of, anyway.

"Castor?"

He turned, everything in him relaxing as he recognized the voice. Darius. He grabbed the younger man in a hug. Darius always knew how to make his day brighter.

He pulled away, his brown eyes searching Castor's. "Is it true? Is there a probe?"

"You know that kind of information is above my pay grade." But it didn't keep Darius from prodding. He asked a lot of questions.

Darius looked around the busy hallway before giving Castor what was clearly intended to be a meaningful look.

Shit, the man thought Castor was acting coy because they were in public.

If there was something to tell, he would, like he *always* did. But he just didn't know anything. Castor wasn't close to many people since he'd left Earth, which was a horrible feeling. Living on Earth might have been crappy, but he had family and friends there, people he was close to and wanted to impress. There? Out in the black? He might as well be invisible.

Except with Darius.

The lights above the corridor headwalls flashed yellow, putting the station in alert mode.

Darius noted the alarm and grimaced, tipping his head to the side. His expression was pretty close to a pout.

"I have to go, emergency yellow." Normally, that meant return to stations or quarters, except he was on the Emergency Response team.

"Of course. I'll see you at home later." Darius leaned in to press a kiss to his lips.

Sometimes that man was like a child, but he couldn't help but feel love for him. Love? No. Admiration? Not quite that either. They were still in the awkward, what-do-we-feel-for-each-other stage of the relationship. "I'll see you later."

Darius sighed. "Yes. We will, and we'll continue *this* later."

Castor chuckled and turned on his heel, heading toward the command center.

When he arrived, Commander Walker paced back and forth in the small secure room used as the command center on End's Reach Station. She was short but lithe and she wasn't a woman anyone wanted to piss off. She'd made commander with good reason.

The other six members of the team filed in and took their seats, looking to Walker to brief them.

"The transmission is accurate," Walker began. "A probe is en route to the station. The details contained within are essential to the expansion movement of the human race. We have reason to believe the Outsystem Alliance has been coordinating these True Voice transmission hacks. I know that's not exactly a surprise to anyone. Those terrorists are almost as bad as the Earther Nationalists."

Castor didn't *quite* agree with that. True Voice had inconvenienced people. Earther Nationalists killed them.

"Each of you will take a quadrant of the station. We can't allow an uprising. Not now. I want every hatch opened, every cabin inspected, every storage compartment scanned. This kind of hacking requires access to technology and we're going to find it. Tonight."

An explosion boomed through the command station, something powerful enough to briefly disrupt the station's stabilizers.

Castor rose, weightless for a moment, before the gravitational controls overcompensated and pulled him to the ground.

The Emergency Response team stared at each other for a split second before rising to their task. *They* were the Emergency Response team and there was obviously an emergency.

Castor regained his footing and stumbled out the door into the hall where sparks flew from control panels embedded in the walls and even more people had flooded into the public areas to find out what they could about the disruption. He pushed his way through the crowd, even knocking a few people over as he rushed toward the flight deck; his assigned quadrant and a likely location for an uprising.

There was also a good chance that was where the explosion had come from. His day was turning out to be exciting at least.

Yeah. Now, if he could just survive the excitement.

II

Castor jogged down the main ramp on his way to the flight deck. A mass of civilians swarmed toward him.

Armed guards surrounded and passed his approach. Static filled the air and the tiny hairs on the back of his neck rose.

One of several pilot fighters beside him exploded.

Castor flew across the room and against one of the steel beams supporting the massive dome above his head. His ears rang with pain. Debris from the cruiser flew through the air. He hunkered in place, covering his head with his arms.

Most of the civilians had managed to clear the area, so the only people left—for the most part—were blue-uniformed soldiers.

The man who spoke, though, was wearing a different uniform; black and red of the Outsystem Alliance. His deep voice bellowed out, cutting through the chaos. "Who's in charge here?" He leaped on top of one of the cranes used to access the top of fighter jets.

Shit. That was probably Castor. One of the lowest ranking officers on this station, but...still an officer. He rose to his feet, his hands raised. "That would be me."

The leader turned his head and looked at Castor with a critical eye. "You." He flicked his eyebrows. "Okay." He gestured to someone behind Castor.

Someone grabbed him by the arms and pulled him backward before throwing a cover over his head. He had no idea where they were going. He only knew they weren't on the same level anymore.

When his captor ripped away the cover, Castor found himself in a small room with at least twenty similarly black and red uniformed men and women.

"Lieutenant Castor, what do you know about the incoming probe?" The tall man wore welding goggles and a scarf around his neck, making it hard to distinguish any characteristics beyond his height and booming voice.

How did they know his name? "What do I call you?"

The man smiled and straddled a chair. "Dumaur."

That name sounded familiar, but Castor didn't know from where.

"What do you know?"

"Nothing."

"Don't lie to me. You're there as the leader of the Emergency Response team."

"So? That doesn't mean I get information."

"Our intel says different."

Castor shrugged. "Sorry." These guys pissed him off. They killed when killing didn't need to happen, when lives could be saved. He wasn't giving Dumaur anything.

"We could use a guy like you on the inside."

"It's not going to happen."

"You have us wrong."

"Do I?"

Dumaur narrowed his eyes. "You seem like a decent guy."

He was obviously a bad judge of character.

"We're fighting for the survival of the human race."

"So are we." But he didn't *believe* Dumaur was fighting for *life* when he *killed* so easily. Yeah, sure. Castor was in the military, but that didn't make him a war monger.

It just meant he liked to eat and drink water and breathe air.

"The military cannot be allowed to be the sole holders of information regarding the human race."

Castor didn't necessarily disagree with him, but he wasn't going to *say* that out loud. "You're better?"

Darius' lithe body and dark hair slipped between two large thugs to Castor's left. "Please listen to him. People are desperate."

Darius? His sweet, innocent Darius? *He* was a part of this? Just…how? Why?

"I'm here to make this easier." Darius reached for him.

Castor recoiled, bumping into a woman standing close behind with a pulse blaster. "Easier?"

"We need…" Darius took a step back.

Into the folds of the enemy. Castor couldn't *believe* his eyes.

"We need your help."

"I can't be a part of this."

"Baby," Darius said, his voice low. "Events have already fallen into place. They're already—" He closed his eyes.

What the hell was Castor supposed to say to that?

"We're out of time."

Castor opened his mouth to speak.

A flash of light shot through the port window. It looked like it was from Earth's position, but that—that wasn't possible. A light flash that large that could be seen from End's Reach?

But then the reality punched him in the gut. The light from that blast was almost five hours old, meaning whatever had happened to create that was already…

III

It was time to leave. Castor struggled through the crowd in the small room, shoving his way through the bodies of insurgents who had put him in an impossible position.

They didn't stop him. Why not? Because of Darius?

Castor paused at the door to glance at Darius.

His lips were set in a grim tight line and he held his hands together in front of him. "At least think about it. We need you."

"I don't work with murderers." And if they'd known about what had happened on Earth, then that meant they had to be in on it. And that meant...

An explosion that big? How many were dead? The planet? A continent?

Commander Walker would know what had happened.

The halls were eerily empty. Unlike after the transmission, no one had come out into the common areas. He ran to the lift. They had brought him to maintenance level seven.

The lift took him directly to Command Center where a defeated and tired looking Walker sat.

She didn't even look up at him.

"Commander," he said quietly, stepping into position. "What happened? I saw the flash."

"We should wait. The others will need to know, and I don't want to say it more than once if I don't have to."

He couldn't—that wasn't acceptable. "I had family...on Earth. Is it..." He shook his head. He didn't want to say it out loud.

Commander Walker's eyes sharpened. "Where?"

"What do you mean?"

"Where on Earth is your family?"

That meant it wasn't the entire planet. His family could still be fine. "Colorado," he said in a tight whisper.

"Oh."

Dread filled Castor's entire body.

Walker let her head fall to her chest. "The Earthers attempted to use terraforming technology. A misguided attempt to fix what we've done down there."

A terra—no. You didn't terraform a living planet. Everyone *knew* that.

"They focused on the Rocky Flats, but..."

"But I saw the blast. It had to be...massive."

"Yes. The blast broke through the atmosphere. Colorado is gone. Most of Wyoming and Utah, too. It will be generations before Colorado is habitable again, if ever."

Castor stumbled backward. His sister lived there...*had* lived there. And her kids. His cousins. Everyone he'd known growing up.

"I have to..."

"Of course," Walker said, looking at him with sympathetic eyes and a pity he didn't want.

The rest of the Emergency Response Team arrived in a swell of voices and stomping boots. The sound banged round him, an assault on his ears. Walker stood to explain the destruction the Earthers wrought on the planet, but he slipped out the doors, the calming swish of them closing behind him the only sound he heard.

His home was gone.

His relationship was a lie.

The military had intel they weren't sharing with the governments or the organized people.

Everything was falling apart.

He wished he'd been planet side for the disaster. To die with his feet firmly planted in the dirt. Did his sister see it coming? Was it like a cascading atomic bomb that spread out from the epicenter or was it so fast she died instantly, in peace? Did she have a chance to hold her children before the end?

The metal under his feet vibrated and with each step, its unnatural hardness radiated up his leg, pounding his bones together. The lights shone brightly and blinded him in the hall. He found himself standing in front of his quarters, his chest tight. Darius would be inside. Maybe. Did he know about the planet?

Castor couldn't remember if he'd ever even told Darius where he was from. Would it be just another piece of the puzzle for Darius to use against him? He didn't even know the man, did he?

He couldn't catch his breath, he needed a moment without the insanity, without people or politics. He wanted to go back to watching the clock until the end of his shift then getting a few drinks in the commons. He wanted a breath of fresh air.

Castor made his way to the closest airlock and sat on the floor, letting the door seal behind him. With the press of just one button, he could be outside, out in the void, the black. Just one button and it would all be over.

In training, they'd told them that dying from exposure in space really wasn't the worst way to go.

A person could live for almost two minutes out there. He'd lose consciousness quickly, but if someone found him and re-pressurized his body, he could recover. The vacuum would kill him before the cold, but he wouldn't feel any of it.

An EVU hung against the wall.

Castor slipped it on, sealing himself in and for a moment, considered not tethering himself to the station, just floating out there for as long as the EVU had air then succumbing to the black.

In the end, he was a coward. Always had been.

He attached the tether to the suit, stowed anything loose, and depressurized the airlock before opening the doors. Unauthorized spacewalks weren't permitted, were even punishable by court-martial, but Castor doubted anyone would care. They certainly wouldn't notice he'd disappeared. There were much more important things to focus on.

He pressed the release button and the hatch whirled open. The station was getting old. The last of the air propelled him out into the open and for a moment, Castor felt free. The airlock faced away from the planet and he looked out at the open space. No moon, no Earth, no people. He could be anywhere. He could be the lone surviving human in the universe and that idea lifted a weight off his shoulders that had been holding him down even in zero-g.

The station rotated, and the slow movement soothed Castor's soul until Earth came into view. Castor pressed the control panel on his forearm and brought up the ocular enhancement option for his shield. This way he could see what had become of Earth. A splash of brown covered most of North America. The toxic gasses the terraforming would have released spread through the air like wildfire. This one desperate act could kill off the entire continent, if not the whole world.

And he floated like he didn't have a care in the world.

It was time to decide what kind of man he really was.

IV

Castor repressurized the airlock and pulled off his helmet. Immediately, it rang with a blasting voice in his comm.

"Castor. Where are you? Get your ass to command center now."

"On my way." He pulled the suit off, leaving it on the floor of the airlock. All the peace and resolve he'd found outside sloughed away like mud in the rain.

In the command center, the Emergency Response Team hovered around a single console.

"Everyone non-essential out," Walker bellowed.

Castor turned to go.

"Not you, Castor. You're here."

Since when had Castor become essential? *Fuck.*

"This transmission just came through. So far, our systems show no signs of hacking, but we're on the clock before the Outsystem Alliance breaks in and transmits another broadcast."

"What does it say?" Higgins asked.

"Listen."

This is the Helo Odysseus *transmitting through secure channels for End's Reach Military Command only. Command, the jump technology worked, and we arrived safely in system 693.14. We have the first planet eligible for terraforming. All of our tests reveal that there's minimal local vegetation which might survive the process, and there are no sentient species. The crew here has taken to calling it "Man's Joy" or "Joy" for short. You're clear to load up the equipment and move out!* Helo Odysseus *out.*

The first colonizable, terraformable world. The discovery changed everything. No longer were they bound to an Earth which only an hour ago had been contaminated even further. The fallout of the Earthers' failed experiment couldn't be anticipated, but this other planet—Joy—it could be a new home. A new beginning.

The room filled with chatter as even the most stoic of military professionals tittered at the possibilities this transmission presented.

Walker tapped the comm board with her thumb. "Needless to say, I don't want word of this getting out." She passed her gaze over everyone, pressing the command. "We need to load the ships with the terraforming chemicals and machinery and get them off station before the Outsystem Alliance has a chance to broadcast this publicly. If word gets out, we'll have a rush on the ships. We can't take everyone and the necessary equipment."

"What about loading all the equipment onto one ship and sending it in advance?" Higgins asked. "Then we could get there that much sooner!"

Castor was struck with the uncharacteristic desire to punch someone.

"It's too heavy. We can't skybreak with that load. We've been over this a million times. Three ships, three crews, three jumps through the push. It's the only way."

Delagio, the head engineer, wore a look of exacerbation. "I need forty-eight hours to get the ships flight ready."

"You have six." Walker stood and pulled down her uniform jacket, leaving it crisp and pristine as if she hadn't had the worst day in the history of End's Reach Station.

"That soon?" Higgins practically vibrated out of his uniform with excitement.

"Use whatever you need. Pull crews from other duties. Deploy the mechs, whatever it takes. Tell no one and get it done. I will begin making a roster of ship's crews but make no mistake. Just because you're in this room doesn't mean you're going. I need people here with me who can keep the station running."

"You aren't going?" He couldn't imagine staying there. He didn't want to live out his entire life on a *station*. If he had a chance…

"No." Walker's expression was pinched at the eyes. "My place is here. Now get to it."

Another planet beckoned him. He knew what Walker had said, and he'd done nothing in his life to make him worthy of seeing what lay beyond the Sol system, but he needed to go. Desperation clawed at him. His family was dead. The earth would be dead soon. There was nothing left for him. Except Darius.

Castor trailed behind the excited men and women who went about their jobs getting the ships ready for deployment. His position was relatively unnecessary. The rations and supplies for the ships simply needed to be pulled from storage and loaded on board. With a few taps on his comm, he had the mechs pulling what he needed and taking them to the flight deck. It would be at least an hour before he needed to be there to supervise the load.

He returned to his room to find Darius sitting on the edge of their bed.

"I didn't know if you'd come back here."

Castor didn't know what do to. Yell at him? Demand to know if he *knew?* To cry to—his…sister—he gulped a breath.

Darius pulled Castor into his arms, burying his nose in his neck.

Castor held onto him, his only lifeline. "Tell me you didn't know, that you weren't behind this."

"It wasn't us. Civilians trying to…fix a dying planet."

"But you knew."

Darius pulled away, gripping the back of Castor's neck. "We tried to get as many out as we could."

"My family?" Castor knew it was a dumb question.

Darius shook his head and Castor's sanity crumbled just a little bit more. "I'm so sorry. I didn't know in time. We saved as many as we could, but the effects are spreading. Even our attempts to rescue people might not be enough. Did you hear the transmission? Is there hope?"

Castor nodded, numb. "They found a planet to terraform."

"We have to get word to Dumaur." Darius pulled away and strode toward the door.

"No, we can't tell anyone. Don't you understand? This is the first mission out. It has to succeed. We can't risk the Outsystem Alliance sabotaging it."

"Sabotaging? Have you really bought into the propaganda so completely that you think I could be involved in a terrorist group? The whole point is that the military cannot be allowed to control portal travel. They can't create an entire world as a military outstation. The rest of humanity deserves to have a voice."

"Remember, planets are big. And they will, of course. The second wave of settlement ships will be civilian."

Darius shook his head and looked sadly at Castor. "You can't really believe that. How do you think the Earthers got the terraforming technology? They don't have the science to build it themselves. The amount of power it would take to set off a terraformer is more than they could manage on their own. They had to have access to fusion or some other power source. Where would they get that? Only the military has access to such things."

"Are you suggesting the military—"

"Armed the Earthers. Yes." Darius nodded sadly. "The military you have so much faith in are the same people responsible for so many deaths."

"My sister... her kids..."

Darius reached out for his hand, taking it in both of his and bringing it to his lips. "Help us. Help us infiltrate those ships. Help us make sure the expansion movement isn't a military installment but a representation of all people."

"Is humanity worth it? Are any of us worth saving?"

"You are, Xavier Castor."

"So are you, Darius Zervek."

V

It took almost three hours for Castor to distribute the supplies as directed, all the while slipping members of the Outsystem Alliance onto *Tallion*, the first colony ship bound for another planet. An hour before launch and the other ships were just beginning to load.

"We need to launch before Walker begins boarding the ship." Castor paced on the flight deck, speaking to Darius over his comm.

"What do we need to do?" Darius rested his hand on Castor's arm.

"I need the dock lockdown code, which I can get from Command center, but there's no way to open the airlock with so many people in here. They'll all be sucked out into the black."

"We knew there may be casualties," Darius spoke with a calm certitude Castor had never heard before.

"Casualties, yes, but not the entire flight crew."

"Only the people on the deck. The rest of the station will be fine. We don't want to take any lives, but we're doing this for humanity. For the greater good. We do what we must. Go get the code."

Darius clicked off his comm.

Castor swore as he kicked a floor crawling mech.

Soldiers and servicemen scurried throughout the flight deck. No one noticed when Castor slipped onto the lift to sneak into the Command Center. Not only would none of them have any business there, but who would care what the lieutenant in charge of freeze-dried meats did? His invisibility once again served to keep him from being noticed.

This time, though, part of him wanted to be caught, to be forced to confess what he had done. He could tell Walker and secure himself a place on the ship. Fuck Darius for putting him in this position. But he had no doubt the Outsystem Alliance would fight to the last life before giving up that ship, and so would Walker.

The command center was blessedly abandoned, allowing Castor to log in through the secure console and access the launch codes needed for all three ships without being seen. Maybe he could have them all lockdown to launch. Only the people already on board would be able to travel, but it was better than killing anyone on the flight deck. The logistics of it all were more than he could process, and things were happening too fast. He wanted to be back outside, dangling by a tether and floating above the Earth.

"What are you doing up here, Lieutenant?" Commander Walker barked.

Castor jumped right out of his skin. *Shit.* "Just, ahh, making sure I have the most current roster."

"That will be transmitted to you when its finalized. We're keeping the list locked down so people who aren't selected don't have time to protest."

"Of course," Castor said. "That makes a lot of sense. Sorry about that. Just trying to be proactive."

If Walker hadn't been preoccupied, she'd have known he was up to something. He had never been proactive about anything in his career. But as he shuffled passed her, she patted him on the shoulder. "Good job, Castor. Thanks for keeping things running smoothly."

His throat closed up and no word could escape. He wanted to confess. He wasn't a good soldier or a good man. All he did was nod and make his way back down to the flight deck.

When he arrived, one of the crewmen caught his eye and headed his way. He didn't want to talk or make nice or pretend everything was copacetic, but appearances mattered.

"You hear what they're calling the new planet?"

"No, what?" Castor asked without looking up from his vidscreen.

"Terra Joy. It means a Joyful Earth."

"Yeah, I get it. Super clever. You guys should write a book."

The crewman frowned but when Castor didn't continue, he wandered away.

Would that man die if Castor followed Darius' plan? Could he live with that?

Before he could think too deeply about the possibilities, Castor slipped inside the ship *Tallion*, past the giant mechs loading the terraforming machinery. Creating a new planet out of nothing was the work of a God. Did humanity deserve it after what they'd done to their own world? His grief for his sister stirred but he shoved it down, needing to focus on the work at hand. He was determined to see Terra Joy, to step foot on a new planet. This would be the beginning of a whole new life.

"Did you get it?" Darius asked. The Outsystem Alliance's people had been slowly infiltrating the flight deck crew and sneaking on board, filling the ship to capacity with their own scientists, engineers, and leaders. Castor recognized many of the faces around him, having never suspected them of treason. How much of his life had he sleep walked through?

"I got all three." He handed the vidscreen over.

"Excellent! Then we can load more of our people and lock the military out."

"No," Castor stepped into an excited Darius' space. "That's not what we agreed. One ship to offset the military's control. One ship to make sure freedom expanded with the colonization of the stars. No more."

Darius gave him a mocking smile with a cruel edge Castor had never seen before. "It's so cute when you think you're in charge. Like when you thought I was the one so in love with you, I'd die if you left me, and when you thought you were the one making the decision to help us as opposed to being the pawn you've been all along."

"Darius?" Confusion jumbled Castor's thoughts. What had he just said? Why did the young man he'd been with for three years suddenly look so much older, so much meaner?

"These codes are the key to everything. We will rule the universe now. Not the simpering military."

"This isn't the plan." Castor struggled, his mind two steps behind Darius' words.

"This was always the plan."

Overhead, an alarm sounded. It blared through the flight deck: code orange, security breach. On the vid screen, they watched guards march into the open space and line the walls. Commander Walker was escorted in last.

Castor and Darius watched as she appraised the preparations. The guards held their guns at the ready, not quite poised for attack, but ready should the need occur.

"What do we do?" Castor wiped his sweaty palms on his thighs.

"You go out there, misdirect them while we finish preparations and then when you're back and things are calm, we'll take off before they even have a chance to question us. Can you do that? Can you save us?" Darius' eyes were round and bright. The sweetness Castor had always seen in him returned, making him question what the man had said before.

He nodded and made his way off the *Tallion* but as soon as his feet touched the flight deck, the cargo bay door began to close.

VI

"Darius!" Castor screamed as the overhead alarm turned from orange to red. "What are you doing? Darius!"

"What is the meaning of this, Lieutenant Castor?" Walker approached but the *Tallion*'s engine roared, making it impossible to answer.

He grabbed the powerful woman's arms and shoved her out of the way of the initial combustion from the ship's thrusters.

"We have to get out of here!" he screamed.

"We'll do no such thing! Who is piloting that ship?"

Castor hung his head. "Darius Zervek. My partner."

"You took the access codes!" The betrayal in her eyes was almost more than he could take, but the alarm overhead was replaced with a countdown for the bay doors.

Castor's ears popped as the room began to depressurize around them in preparation for takeoff. "We have to get out of this room or onto one of the ships. They're going to open the doors. We can't stop them now."

"Like hell we can't," Higgins said raising his gun.

"No!" The blast would simply ricochet off the ship. "You can't stop this, but you might kill someone. Commander Walker, give the order, load all your men on those ships now."

"We're leaving so many behind."

"It's that or let them die. The bay doors have sealed with the depressurizing. We're trapped."

Every human on the flight deck flooded into one of the two remaining military controlled ships, piling in on top of supplies that hadn't been secured yet and technology they didn't understand. As the computer counted down, the cargo doors lifted, sealing everyone inside.

"They won't want us to follow. They wanted to take over all three ships, not just the one," Castor blurted to a furious Walker.

"And you helped them."

"And look what happened!" He practically screamed the words, unable to keep his emotions and exhaustion in check any longer. "He betrayed me. He manipulated me."

"Because you're weak." Walker turned on her heel and headed toward the cockpit.

When the flight deck doors finally opened, all the materials not secured down were sucked into open space. The two military ships began take-off preparations, but the *Tallion* was all ready to go.

Castor watched as the ship carrying his lover took off toward the jump ring that would take them to Terra Joy.

"They'll destroy the ring." He gasped, realizing too late what the plan had been all along. "They'll do anything to keep the military from colonizing beyond Sol."

"They wouldn't, the ring is our only access to all of the exploration teams and scientists working throughout the galaxy."

"Exactly."

Commander Walker issued commands at the pilot and the ship took off, hard and fast out into the black. "We have to get there before they do. We must get through that ring. Higgins, send a transmission back to End's Reach explaining what is happening. There's no telling if we'll survive or when we'll be able to get a transmission through."

Higgins nodded and got to work while Castor watched, horrified as the telltale lights of *Tallion's* weapons systems came online.

The lasers narrowly missed Castor's ship, the pilot expertly dipping and accelerating toward the ring. They fired more weapons, but these weren't warships, just simple cargo vessels reinforced to survive the push. Unfortunately, that meant that when the second military vessel took a direct hit, the impact was enough to throw it into a tailspin, pushing it off the trajectory of the ring. One more hit and the third ship exploded, debris flying through the darkness like stars.

"We're not going to make it," Castor yelled.

Commander Walker glared at him as a familiar voice came from the overhead speakers.

This is the voice of the people. The only free transmission dedicated to serving all of humanity. Our truth is your truth.

The military has lied to you. There is a planet available for terraforming in system 693.14. They have attempted a covert mission to conquer this new planet for themselves, setting up a military installation as the first colonization effort of humanity. The Outsystem Alliance refuses to sit by and allow this to happen. We have commandeered a ship and are currently en route to the new planet: Terra Joy.

We promise you the truth, and we have delivered. Rise up, fight for humanity's right to rule ourselves. We will be waiting for you on the other side.

Without truth, hope is lost.

Castor's stomach fell. Darius. The cadence of the voice, the deep scratch that came through even after the voice masking. It had been Darius all along.

A Word From P.K. Tyler:

Exodus Sol is from the Black System Legends Universe. It's a collective of three authors, two of which are USA Today Bestselling Authors. We write individually and co-author as we explore a new universe together.

P.K. Tyler brings the heart to our stories. Her passion for politics and social equality bring an important element to our work. She believes love is the answer, and enjoys showing you people fighting who they are to become someone better. It only takes one person to change the universe. Do you *See* that heart?

K.S. King gives us the mechanics. Well, he *is* a mechanic who *loves* to play and tinker and blow stuff up. We would say "not literally," but that would be a lie. He keeps our universe real. He's the first one to say, "It doesn't work that way." He's also our fight-scene expert.

Frankie Blooding likes to take hard-to-understand people and bring readers into their head. She enjoys showing that the jerk you can't stand is a human being. So, maybe he only has *one* feeler, but he *has* it. She also loves action scenes, though her favorite scenes are when characters are talking to each other around tables. We have to keep her on a tight leash.

You can find out more about our universe at blacksystemlegends.com

Deep Throw 1
Terry R. Hill

IN THE FALL OF 2017, Earth was buzzed by the interstellar asteroid "Oumuamua." In this alternate history, NASA teamed up with the Department of Defense to develop a rapid launch and rendezvous capability as part of a high-risk rapid launch mission to explore the solar system.

"Tether impact in ten seconds. Five. Four. Three. Two. One…Attachment confirmed. All parameters within expected values," reported Dr. Asha Anand, the most junior of the Deep Throw 1 (DT1) crew.

"Commander, real-time tether harpoon telemetry appears to validate our radar measurements of the asteroid's rotation rate. However, our relative velocity is greater than expected," said second in command, Yolanda Baker.

"Assessment?" asked Commander Maria Riboli.

"Stand by…it's going to be close," Yolanda replied.

"Within margins?" asked Maria.

"I don't think—"

"Yolanda, yes or no, thirty seconds. Go or no go!"

"Keep your panties on, I'm running the numbers again."

"Yolanda…"

"Window closing in fifteen seconds," announced Asha.

"Yolanda!"

"Abort! Velocity's too high."

"Abort Asha, abort. Sorry, ladies. Maybe next time," Maria said.

"Maria!"

"What is it, Asha?"

"I'm showing a negative release of the tether."

"What? Are we getting good telemetry?" asked Maria.

"Data looks good. Seeing higher impact loads than expected. Telemetry looks good too, just not what we want to see. Probably damaged the pyro disconnect switches," replied Yolanda. In her fifties, she was the oldest of the three crewmembers and the most experienced with the system's design, especially the tether system and the primary vehicle systems. The tether system was critical to mission success, but now everything was in doubt.

"Okay. Options? Can we disconnect it on our end?" barked Maria.

A cold shiver ran down Yolanda's neck as she finished the math in her head.

"Can't do it. Not enough time for an EVA. The relative velocity between us and that rock is close to eighty kilometers per hour. That's too fast. The manual disconnect was a fail-safe for separation to go home. Best we can do now is have faith in the engineers," replied Yolanda.

"Shit," muttered Maria. "Okay, button up. Face masks closed. Let's hope those engineers were as conservative as their rep. Begin reeling in the tether."

The tether system was designed to fire a harpoon tipped with a high-energy laser. If the preliminary analysis of the asteroid was correct, it was mostly metal—the laser would soften it up, allowing deep penetration and secure attachment by the tether. The several-kilometer tether would be reeled back to take up the slack as the asteroid overtook them. As it passed, the tether would be released again. A braking system would gradually slow the unwinding tether and, in turn, speed up their vehicle. Once the relative velocity between spacecraft and asteroid was minimized, they would rendezvous and soft dock. At least, that was the plan.

"Retraction underway and looking good. Approaching thirty thousand RPM," Asha reported.

Increasing strain on the retraction motor in the cabin was audible. The amount of energy stored in the tether system defied imagination—be it the kinetic capabilities like the reeling in and out of the tether, the amount of energy the braking system had to absorb, or the sheer strength of the structure required to handle the loads resulting from acceleration to speeds three times greater than any human spacecraft had ever traveled. None of this was lost on Yolanda. The three of them, the first all-female crew, heck the first crew period, to perform a deep-space exploration mission, were to be the first to test this incredible technology for real.

Please, God, let it work, she prayed. At her age, there wasn't much that still scared her. But this? This was enough to help her get some old-time religion again.

Minutes passed as the interstellar rock raced toward them. The tether retraction system continued to perform as expected.

"Oumuamua," Asha reported, referring to the asteroid designated 1I/2017 U1, "will pass us with half a kilometer margin in thirty seconds."

Half a kilometer, that wasn't much room.

Yolanda was present during the design phase when the length of the tether, which drove the system's mass, was factored by the size of the launch vehicle and, in the end, dictated how close to the metaphorical speeding bullet they had to be. Relatively speaking, they would have a very large and tumbling rock passing them at seventy-three times the speed of sound. Only the engineers of the Apollo era had the audacity to attempt something like this. And because of funding issues since then, that was the technology they were using. The hubris involved was beyond laughable, but here she was and not alone.

"Here it comes…" said Yolanda, quietly puckering in her suit, looking out the forward-facing window where the rock would soon be appear.

"Tether system unlocked and ready to spool out," Asha reported.

Without sound or vibration, in an instant, the massive, abnormally cylindrical body blurred past them, and was only a small light retreating into the distance.

The ship jerked violently, pulled by the tether now pointed toward Oumuamua and screaming like an angry banshee as it unwound.

"Shit!" exclaimed Maria. "Report."

"RPM's are in the red, but we're okay for now," Yolanda replied. "Engaging forced-breathing assistance and tether braking system. Hold on!"

The next few moments were critical and potentially deadly as the braking system slowed the tether reel, resulting in rapid acceleration of their vehicle to match the asteroid's velocity.

The air escaped her lungs momentarily as she was slammed back into her seat. Her body fought the sudden rush of air forced into her lungs, and would have thrown itself into a fit of gagging and coughing if the pressure was lower. The ship would do the breathing for them for the next few minutes.

The acceleration readings raced past one-g, two-gs, three-gs, four-gs…they would black out soon. Things were already closing in and getting dim. *Must hold on… Four and a half g's… Breathe! Breathe! Must… hold… on!*

"Commander!" Yolanda called over the comm system.

"Go ahead!" Maria replied over the whining of the tether echoing inside her helmet.

"We're running out of tether!"

"Increase braking."

"Can't! Already redlining. That much time over five gs would kill us."

"Dead either way!" Maria shouted.

Yolanda pushed the button to execute and was once again slammed into her seat. Four gs…four and a half…five… The seams of her space suit bit into her skin and every jitter and bump threatened to crush her bones.

Ahhh!!

Tunnel vision had narrowed her world to a soda straw hole as she attempted to stay conscious to monitor the tether.

It's not going to be enough!

It would be close, but a difference of a couple hundred kilometers per hour when you run out of rope is still fatal.

Please let this not be the end! Must tell the commander...

She could force no words past the impossible pressure on her chest. It was very likely the other two were unconscious anyway.

Here it was. The end of the line. Literally. In three...two...one.

NASA had been watching for interstellar asteroids for some time. The possibility existed that debris from other solar systems could be flung out into the cosmos during any of the incomprehensibly violent things that happen out there. And any such rock could, in theory, be captured by our sun's gravitational field and pulled in and pass through our solar system. This was one of those asteroids.

In the early days of NASA, after the Apollo program wound down and as the Space Shuttle program was underway, some of Von Braun's team began to think in terms of deep space exploration. They understood what it took just to get humans traveling fast enough to get to the moon in three days. It was also understood those speeds were nowhere near fast enough to make human exploration of our solar system a reality. The distances, the time, and the amount of fuel required was beyond what was possible.

So, they began thinking outside of the box. What if they didn't have to accelerate humans to god-like velocities? What if they could hitch a ride? What if there were asteroids that were big enough, fast enough, and traveled close enough to Earth that we could catch a ride with them? NASA could then attach to these rocks long enough to reach the desired velocity, separate, and travel on to the desired destination at a fraction of the un-aided time.

Comets falling in from the Ort Cloud generally crawled along on average at about a quarter of the speed of the Apollo 10 crew going to the Moon. They would need something faster which didn't require stealing velocity from large-planet flybys. Interstellar asteroids were the answer. That was how Project Deep Throw began.

To pull off such a mission, everything had to be perfect—but the payoff would be well worth it. NASA had been ready, and when Oumuamua was detected, the wheels were put into motion. Deep Throw 1 had previously been launched and tethered to the International Space Station early in the assembly phase, and had been in deep mothballs since. As soon as the agency knew the conditions were right with Oumuamua, the crew of three were activated and launched to the space station manifested as an unmanned resupply. Once they were onboard, with a hydroponics food module connected to their vehicle, they lit the fuse and were on their way.

The mission had to be secret. The risk-averse public that dictated policy wouldn't tolerate the odds. So, in dark corners of Washington, the decision was made. Launch in secret, and if it appeared the mission would be a success, declare victory and turn the crew into worldwide heroes. Asking forgiveness was always easier than asking for permission.

The general idea was to let the asteroid tow them at its much faster speed as it headed out to the cosmos. When they got closer to Jupiter, they would separate from Oumuamua, use the planet's gravity to slow down a little, and come screaming back in towards the Earth. Nine-month mission, tops. Just like a tour of the space station. Easy peasy!

Wha-?
Who?
What's going on?

Pain. Lights. Flashing.

Ah! My head! Blood in helmet!
Focus! What the hell are all the alarms going off in my helmet?
Okay. Still breathing. That's good.
Shit.

The display panel looked like a possessed Christmas tree. Flashing red and yellow lights everywhere.

Yolanda wasn't pinned to her seat anymore, so either the tether had been ripped from the ship or they were still attached and had somehow matched Oumuamua's velocity.

A quick look left and right confirmed the other two were still unconscious. Sparks erupted from someplace behind and bounced around the cabin until they burned out. Yep, they'd lost pressure containment in the cabin, which was verified by the fact that her suit was pressurized. How long had they been out? Glancing out the forward windows, it was obvious they were in a tumble...

What was that? Looks like a rock, a big one. The tether must have held. But at what cost?

"Maria! Wake up, Maria!" Yolanda shouted, immediately regretting it as her voice echoed in her helmet. After hitting the quick release of the multi-point harness, she reached over and shook the commander and tried again. Maria came to with a start, flailing at unseen monsters.

"Maria, you're okay. You're okay. Calm down. You're okay!"

"What happened? What's going on? Sitrep?"

"Asha is unconscious. Cabin is depressurized. Multiple system alarms, and we seem to be tumbling near the asteroid. I need your help to kill the tumble while I turn off some of these alarms and figure out how bad things are," she reported.

"Okay. Okay. Good. I got it. Figure out what's going on with the ship. See if Asha is okay."

Yolanda looked over at Asha. No visible blood in the helmet. She punched a few buttons on the display in front of her. There was a heartbeat.

"She's alive and stable. She'll keep," Yolanda said.

Now to find out what was going on with the ship. First task: kill the alarms. Three display buttons and one manual switch later, the klaxons blaring through her very soul ceased their incessant alarm. She went through the flight software, error tree by error tree, assessing their status. Thank God she'd taken the initiative to study all the manuals and design drawings, and bugged the engineers who originally designed the vehicle. All those years, they thought she was a bored astronaut taking a mission that would never happen way too seriously.

"Vehicle tumble is canceled out. We've matched the asteroid's rotation and are holding at a quarter kilometer.

The attitude computer is down. I had to fly the damn thing manually," Maria announced.

Yeah, Maria could be a tad obnoxious, but she was one of the best pilots NASA had. She was a recent arrival from the DOD and, thank goodness, a former fighter pilot who was accustomed to regaining control of an aircraft after a blackout. Normal people wouldn't get their head together after something like that 'til they'd had a cup of coffee. But that's about twenty minutes longer than you have in a spiraling fighter.

"Looks like we've been unconscious for over two hours, had a pressure leak in the midsection near the tether reel, and the sudden shock when the tether reeled-out threw the system into automatic shutdown." And thank God for those structural engineers, but it meant that she and Maria would spend quite some time throwing breakers and reinitializing the systems. If they were lucky, they might be able to send a signal back home by the end of the day. Day...whatever that meant now.

"Do we have enough O2 reserves to pressurize the cabin so we can find the leak?" asked Maria.

"Uh... yes, looks like it, if you can get the patch kit ready in advance and are quick about it," said Yolanda.

"Okay, start repressurizing the cabin, Yolanda," Maria ordered.

Moments passed. "Pressure is at 8 psi. High enough to take off your gloves and helmet, but low enough to decrease the leak rate," announced Yolanda.

"So ends today's lesson on vehicle pressure dynamics. Damn engineers," Maria said as she winked at Yolanda and flashed a smile. Maria was good that way. Kept her cool and was able to bring others' stress down too. She popped off her helmet and gloves in a few fluid motions. On the space station, they would have had a sonic detector which could 'hear' the leak. But with mass as a limited resource on this mission, they'd have to do it the old-fashioned way, with their ears.

While Maria worked to find the leak, Yolanda revived Asha. She came to fairly quickly. She'd had longer to sleep it off. The two of them worked to restore power to each of the major legs of the vehicle's primary system. Methodically, they checked each one to make sure no major faults or shorts existed. After the better part of two hours, they were able to restore power to the main computers and begin rebooting life into the vehicle, their home for the next few months.

"Hey! I've found the leak! It's behind one of the panels between crew sleep quarters two and three. Sounds like it's right under the main structure of the tether, just like you said, Yolanda."

"Do you need any help?" asked Asha.

"No, I'm good. It's a tight fit. Just room enough for one hand." Maria readied the metallic patch, put on her left glove and held it while she mixed and applied the two-part epoxy. Not what one really wants to get all over your space suit gloves, but it beat getting that toxic crap all over your hands.

Maria's panicked scream bounced through the vehicle like a rusty chair across a dirty tile floor.

"What's wrong, Maria?" called Yolanda.

"The bulkhead was worse than it looked! My arm was sucked through the hole!"

"What?"

"The hole got bigger and gave way when I was applying the patch. It sucked my arm out!" Weeping sounds came from Maria's direction.

A vacuum formed in the bottom of Yolanda's stomach. Not because of the news, but because one of the toughest women she knew was actually weeping.

When they arrived, the look on Maria's face told them everything they needed to know.

"Get my helmet. Put it on me."

"Why?" asked Asha.

"I have a leak in the arm of my suit somewhere. We can't risk me pulling my arm out...lose too much O2. Suit will give away soon and leak will get larger. Just put on my helmet and it will stop the leak."

"But you'll die!" exclaimed Asha.

"Only way..."

"No. No, it's not," Yolanda stated after a moment of thought. Both looked at her.

"No. I'll put a temporary tourniquet on her arm to hold in the air. We'll all go on umbilicals for O2. We'll use the cabin reclamators to recover as much O2 as possible from the cabin as if we're going EVA, pull Maria out, and then seal off this part of the cabin. They designed this as a safe haven in the event someone needed to stay in the vehicle during an EVA without suiting up. There are no critical systems sensitive to decreased pressure or temperature here, so we just take what we need, seal it off and we'll just have to sleep somewhere else." Sleeping in sacks around the cabin wasn't optimal, but astronauts had been doing it that way for decades. Now who had wasted years of her life studying the schematics? The others stared at her, trying to follow her reasoning.

"Move! Now!" she ordered, jolting them into action. More so Asha since Maria was up to her shoulder and otherwise occupied with being sucked out of the vehicle.

Within moments, they were all connected to the life support system and had helmets on. Maria's lips were turning blue and she was shivering, so it was clear the exposure to deep space was taking its toll on her. It wouldn't be long before hypothermia set in and frozen tissue cell death began.

"On the count of three, pull her away from the bulkhead. Maria, help if you can," Yolanda instructed. Maria mumbled something, but was largely incoherent as she succumbed to hypothermia and possibly blood loss.

With a concerted tug, their commander was pulled free and all three floated backward across the cabin until impacting the wall on the opposite side. Never much fun at any speed.

"Get her in the main cabin, secure her to the wall and get her stabilized while I seal this off and restore cabin pressure," ordered Yolanda.

Less than five minutes later, it was done. "Pressure is good. You can disconnect umbilicals and take off helmets."

Maria was unconscious. Yolanda disconnected the suit at the shoulder and with Asha's help, was able to pull it off. Her left arm was a mess. Ripped and red, and with frozen blood-cicles sticking out like some Halloween nightmare. Where it wasn't red, it was icy blue. And frozen. Solid. She would lose the arm. And if she was lucky, that would be all she lost.

This was bad. Damaged ship, possibly no way to separate from the rock outside, no sleeping quarters, and a commander who likely would lose her arm, and all the while speeding away from the closest hospital, now millions of miles away.

They'd left Earth two months ago and were almost two thirds of the way to Mars, at the critical point when Oumuamua passed from below the plane of ecliptic to above. Doing an orbital plane change was very 'expensive' in terms of fuel, so attaching to the asteroid at just the right time was critical.

Yolanda shook her head to clear it. Whenever life got uncertain, she would always go over the things in her mind that she knew to be hard fact. It was her 'safe' place. Truth be told, that was why she'd gone into engineering. So much of life was subjective and open to interpretation. But not math or engineering. What you thought or believed was irrelevant since the solution worked out the same way, every time.

Asha replaced the tourniquet on Maria's arm now that her suit was removed to keep her from bleeding out as the arm thawed. The communications system was back up, so Yolanda sent a quick update to Mission Control apprising them of the situation. It took almost five minutes for a message to reach Mission Control and another five minutes for a reply to return. The loss of real-time communication was one of the things that made their true isolation most real.

beep beep

The reply from Mission Control had arrived. Yolanda and Asha shared a glance then stared back at the comm display. Did the cabin feel colder? Would their worst fears be confirmed? Maria was half out of it, loaded up on pain meds, and strapped into one of the command chairs.

"Deep Throw 1, this is Mission Control CAPCOM, Michael Fitch speaking. It was good to hear from you after we lost your data feed. Thank you for the vehicle data, our team is analyzing it. We concur with your decision to seal off crew quarters. From the information you've provided on Commander Riboli, the flight surgeons are in agreement that her arm will have to be amputated. They are creating an instructional video of how to perform the operation using the tools you have."

A few seconds of silence had passed before Yolanda realized CAPCOM had stopped talking. A slight shiver raced down her back.

Is that it? A quick check of the comm display confirmed the message was still playing. *What was wrong? What weren't they saying?*

"There were a lot of people happy to hear your voice, Yolanda. We thought we'd lost you."
His voice cracked.

What are you doing, Fitch? CAPCOMs are trained to keep their shit together and not pass along worry or concern to the crew. We...I need you to keep it together!

"The next few days are going to be hard on all of you, but we want you to know that you have all of NASA pulling for you, and doing what we can to make this mission a success and bring you home alive. Try and get some rest. We'll send the video tomorrow morning. Spend the day studying it. You will have only twenty-four hours to do the procedure, according to the docs. Mission Control out."

Sleep was fitful at best. If sleep was even the right word. As promised, the video arrived in the morning and where NASA came up with a cadaver on such short notice was on her short list of things to find out when she returned home. Asha, being a physician, performed the operation quite skillfully using the limited medical equipment available. In many ways, the whole scene reminded Yolanda more of something she would have seen in a 'doctor's office' out West around the turn of the twentieth century, and more brute force and screaming than was experienced these days. Maria passed out on more than one occasion due to the pain—the available meds were no substitute for general anesthesia. But she always regained consciousness, usually screaming. God, the screaming...

To help save on the little antiseptic available for the rest of the mission, the wound was washed with some whiskey Maria had brought along for celebration— something they had planned on doing right about now under very different circumstances—then cauterized using one of the micro-cauteries Asha had brought in her personal bag. Otherwise, they would have had to use torches originally intended for taking samples of the asteroid, which would have been inhumanely brutal. It was unlikely the smell of burning human flesh would ever leave her nose. It wasn't that it was wholly disagreeable, but it was just different enough, in the reality of the situation, for the memory to stick with you.

Maria—miraculously—stabilized quickly and fell into a deep sleep, probably having more to do with her inner strength than it did with either Yolanda's or Asha's skill. But would it be enough?

Six months earlier

It had been a long day of meetings at NASA Headquarters in D.C. The astronaut office sent Yolanda as the representative for the latest round of long-term mission planning to talk to the Senate for approval.

Everyone knew the current administration had no plans to do anything bold, but they had to go through the motions. That was the downside of taking direction from the President instead of Congress. But she couldn't change that. At least she'd get dinner and drinks with a friend on rotation at headquarters.

"So Jon, what's the scuttlebutt around HQ about the latest proposal?" she asked.

"Actually, not much more than you already heard. Everyone knows NASA's not a priority for this administration."

"Disappointing. I was hoping there were some secret missions or new technology being developed. Maybe some news about sending me on an asteroid mission."

The last comment was intended as tongue-in-cheek, but Jon's eyes shot to hers, seeking additional meaning. His face relaxed in a smile.

"No. But funny you should ask. I did hear why they replaced Anderson and Nasgulo with Riboli and Anand for the mission."

"Interesting…" she smiled and leaned in closer. Everyone knew the mission she was assigned to would never fly, but she secretly hoped it would and add some excitement to her largely uneventful life.

"Turns out," he continued, "that the powers that be are very happy with you, and it's been said you have the technical knowledge to pull off the mission, if need be. Anderson got a lucrative job offer with a defense contractor, and Nasgulo got caught diddling the help and is going to 'retire' quietly."

"Seriously? That explains why Nasgulo quit returning my emails. I knew he had a wandering eye, but didn't think he was that reckless. I hope it was worth it. I knew about Anderson's plans. It sounded like a pretty sweet gig." She didn't say anything, but their opinion of her made her smile inside. At NASA, you excelled at your job—it was expected. Only when you either royally screwed something up or improved someone else's screw up did you hear about it. The latter was commonly referred to as "polishing the turd."

"Yeah, the agency is working overtime to keep the story from hitting the media. Don't need any bad press right now." He was quiet for a moment. "So, how do you like working with Riboli?"

"She's fine. She picked up the technical aspects of the mission pretty quick, along with the vehicle piloting sims. Pretty sharp. At first, she was a little intimidating, but she warmed up fairly quickly."

"That's good."

"Why do you ask?"

"Oh, I heard that she got the mission slot after the head of DOD met with the president."

Yolanda laughed heartily.

"What? Aren't you pissed that she didn't earn it like you?"

"Me? Naw. I mean if she wasn't qualified, then yes. But she's a damn good pilot. And besides, Jon, she did earn it. Just not at NASA. How many mission commanders weren't ex-military?"

"Yeah, I guess."

"No guessing about it." Jon was clearly pondering whether to share something.

"What is it, don't you believe me?"

"No, it's not that. Something else."

"Spill the beans!" She bumped his shoulder with hers.

"Okay, but it's about Asha—"

"Oh, I already know she'll be the senior member of the crew when Riboli and I are eventually replaced, if this mission doesn't happen before we retire. She's young, and will grow into it. 'The crew have to be ready to launch at a moment's notice,' isn't that what they always say?"

"Weelll, yes, but that's not the real reason Asha is on the crew."

Jon leaned over to whisper in her ear. It wasn't his words of the discovery of an interstellar asteroid and the activation of their mission that made all the tiny hairs of her body stand on end, but the implications of the real reason they were all picked to go.

A week had passed since the amputation. They continued to maintain cabin pressure within normal limits. Maria had resumed some of her duties, but was still heavily drugged to manage the pain and still had a low-grade fever that needed to be watched carefully. But the fact of the matter was the body of someone in their late forties doesn't heal as fast as someone in their twenties, which was obviously irritating to Maria.

Once the tether winch and systems shipwide were confirmed functional, they began to slowly reel themselves toward the asteroid, occasionally using the maneuvering thrusters to cancel out some of their rotational motion, otherwise physics could be a real bitch.

Life sitting on the asteroid wasn't that different, but the differences were noticeable. Maybe because the immediate horizon didn't change anymore, but the stars rose and set abnormally fast. It seemed like they had solid ground under their proverbial feet, adding to the sense of arrival. Or because looking out the window revealed some very fine divots and textures on this alien interloper. But the light from the sun was fading more and more every day as they flew into deep space faster than any other humans in the history of flight. But to get any real data or answers, they would have to put feet on the surface and get up close and personal with it.

That last part was what had always excited Yolanda about a mission like this. Not just stepping foot on some *etiam firma*, but on something not of our solar system. Something that potentially had a completely different evolutionary process than our own, and to date, the closest opportunity humanity had to contact something from another planetary system...maybe even life.

The long and rather cylindrical asteroid spun strangely on its secondary axis once every seven hours. It was slow enough for them to stay attached to it, but the gravity field was barely detectable and gave them a look back at the sun every seven hours, unlike the space station, where they had a sunrise every ninety minutes. But something else they could see from their observation windows were large sections of relatively smooth surface and large variations in color.

The smooth sections were a blueish grey; the irregular sections were dark brownish-red, almost like dried blood, and consistent with what they knew about material exposed to deep space radiation for very long periods of time. They'd have to perform a spacewalk with the material spectrometer to get a better idea of the chemical makeup and, in turn, an explanation of the variations.

"I'm locked in and ready to extend the arm," announced Yolanda in her space suit and secured to the stanchion at the end of the robotic arm. Due to the very low local gravity, walking would be impossible. The asteroid being very solid, metallic but not magnetic ruled out using electromagnets to compensate. There was no relatively quick or easy way to attach to the surface shy of the high-powered harpoon the ship used.

So, the telescoping robotic arm Yolanda could control from her end would move her in a desired radius around the ship. It wasn't the preferred solution for exploration, but given the constraints and limited time they would be here, it was better than nothing.

"My God…"

"What is it Yolanda? What's wrong?" asked Maria.

"Oh. Oh, nothing's wrong. It's just so…so strange. Amazing. Surreal, I guess." She stole a few guilty moments of pleasure from the very tight spacewalk timeline to take a look around and soak in the moment.

She, a little black girl from a small, poor, Arkansas town, stood on an interstellar object hurtling toward infinity and looked back at humanity's star. How dark it all was, the ground beneath, the endless space. The sun only as bright as a full moon and even so, the Milky Way was visible and overwhelming. Each star an intense, unwavering point of light. This was what NASA was supposed to be about! This was what humans were meant to do! They were different from all the other animals for a reason. And it was clear in that moment, exploring the cosmos was our intended destiny.

"Tick tock, Yolanda. Sun's not getting any brighter," Maria said over the comm loop. She could be a bit of a taskmaster, but she was right. They had trained countless hours on Earth. She needed to stick with the plan. There would never be enough time to answer all the questions they had personally, and certainly not for all the scientists and geologists back home.

"Roger that. Almost at first test site. I'll begin with the reddish, irregular material." She paused, her breaths sounding loud over the comm. "Well, it's relatively soft—

the probe penetrates easily. Running the spectral analysis." A few moments passed. "It looks like this material is generally consistent with non-icy samples we've seen from Ort-cloud comets. I'll take a few samples and move to a smooth spot."

"Yolanda, just so you know, Maria wasn't feeling a hundred percent, so I'm taking over comm while she rests a little," Asha said.

"Understood. Thanks for the heads up. Okay, I'm at the second location. Surface is very regular. The probe cannot penetrate. I can feel a slight texture when I push the probe across the surface, indicating it is very resilient to cosmic debris impact, or was possibly resurfaced via thermal heating when it passed the sun." Geologists constantly drilled these types of observations into her during training, much like the original Apollo astronauts' training.

"I'm deploying the surface grinder to see if I can get below the oxidation." Using the robotic arm, Yolanda was able to apply the necessary pressure to scratch the surface. But whatever it was made of, it wasn't going to give up its secrets easily. After an hour of grinding, she had barely taken a millimeter of material away, but it would probably be enough. It was basically the same color, just ever-so-slightly more reflective, as one would expect of a metal.

"Spectral analysis indicates this is some unknown metallic alloy," Yolanda reported.

"Are you sure?" asked Asha.

"Yes. I've run the test three times in three spots. All the same. This is a problem for the geologist, mineralogist, and materials folks, but I'm not sure how you would get such a large chunk of homogenous metallic alloy naturally... Hey, I'm going to move over to one more smooth area that seems to have a slightly different color."

"Okay, but keep an eye on how much air you have left."

"There is definitely a distinct edge to this other surface. Almost looks like a massive striation. Will start grinding to confirm."

Almost an hour later, she said, "Just from observation, the material underneath looks similar to the other site. Analysis confirms this. However, analysis of the material ground off looks similar, but with higher levels of some of the metallic constituents. Interesting. Not what you would see through normal oxidation or long-term exposure to cosmic or intense solar radiation. I want to get a higher vantage point."

Yolanda maneuvered her end of the arm some thirty meters above the surface.

"Ladies, this is no normal striation."

"What do you mean?" asked Asha.

"I'm seeing curvatures that can't be caused by any natural extrusion or sedimentary processes. Almost looks like—"

"Sorry to interrupt, but you should come back in, Yolanda. Maria's not doing so great. Her fever is up, and she's not making sense." The worry in Asha's voice was clear.

"What are you doing?" Yolanda grabbed Asha's arm as she floated toward the unconscious but fitful commander.

"I'm going to give her another round of antibiotics and antivirals."

"That's from the last case which is supposed to last us 'til we get home."

"I know that! But I'm a doctor. What am I supposed to do, just let her suffer then die?" Yolanda was quiet for a moment.

"Look, if we use it now, there won't be any for later, and the longer we're in space, the more our immune system is compromised and the more we'll need it if something happens."

"Damn it, Yolanda, I know that better than anyone, but that's speculation versus a very sick woman right now!"

Asha pulled a wall strap to resume her progress.

"No," Yolanda insisted.

"Let go!"

"She's right..."

"What?" Asha and Yolanda were stunned.

Maria rasped, "She's right. Save it. If I don't make it, you need the medications to make it home. Two...better than one...or none."

"Maria, just let me try this one last time—"

"No! I'm still the commander. No..."

Yolanda took the med package as she played out the probable scenarios in her mind.

"Besides, pretty sure infection is in the blood now. Not enough antibiotics onboard. I wish I could have gone out there with you. Wish I—" she was interrupted by Asha.

"Maria, you should rest now."

"I wish I could be there when you learn its secrets. And be there when you separate and watch it fly away. I wish I could sit on the stage with you fine ladies when we get back and meet the President..."

"Maria, stop. Rest a little. That's the fever talking," Asha urged.

"No, it's me talking. My mind's clear, for now. I want you to find my ex and tell him that I regret putting my pride before him. Tell him he's a wonderful man who deserved much better than I gave him. He deserved the children I denied him..." Her voice cracked. "Just tell him I'm sorry."

"Maria, stop." Asha dabbed her forehead with a damp cool cloth.

"Yolanda, I can trust you to be levelheaded." Maria's words pierced her. Words like those had always been tossed her direction as compliments, but always stung. They represented her safe, uneventful life driven by wise and safe choices; everyone could count on her doing the right thing while they had the fun. There was always good 'ole dependable Yolanda...

"Yolanda! Can you hear me?" Maria's voice was weak.

She shook the thoughts from her mind. "I'm here. Go on."

"I need you to put me in the crew quarters when I die—"

"Maria—"

"Hear me out. You need every bit of oxygen you have. You can't afford to use it jettisoning me." She was right. As it was, they would have to break into the emergency reserves to make it back home. Maria was starting to drift off.

"Besides, I'll freeze solid pretty quick and if things don't go well, you'll have some extra protein."

"Maria!" Asha was horrified.

"Welcome to deep space. Yolanda?" She was pressing for a commitment Yolanda didn't want to make, for she would honor it despite her own desires. That was just who she was.

"Okay, Maria. Now rest for a little while." Her commander closed her eyes and smiled.

Commander Maria Riboli drew her last breath within the hour, and Yolanda did what was asked of her.

Composing a written message to Mission Control was the only option for Yolanda. They were too far away for a real conversation, which was for the best since there was no way she could have maintained composure. It was a mixed blessing. They didn't have to deal with the constant demands of Mission Control, but they were on their own. No real-time support. They had to solve their own problems.

The extreme distance suited her better anyway. That was probably why she'd been on the list for this mission for so long. Her psych profile said 'a self-starting problem solver who didn't require much social interaction or external gratification.' NASA-speak, meaning ideal for a deep-space mission. The comm lag didn't bother her either. She was probably one of the last astronauts who remembered the world before internet and mobile phones. Back when you had to dig through a physical card catalog to the search for information, or had to wait to find a public pay phone to call someone hoping to catch them near their phone. Yeah, a deep-space mission was pretty much like that.

The reply came the next morning. CAPCOM said everything that was expected. Words to the effect of 'Sorry for your loss. No one back home could really know what it was like for them. They were going to do everything they could to help.' But the last two comments hammered home the reality of their situation.

"Yolanda, some of the material analysis surprised the scientists. We've identified some additional target sites for tomorrow. And Yolanda, I hate to have to say this, but the guys at HQ wanted me to remind you to keep the mission quiet and to absolutely say nothing about what has happened recently. CAPCOM out."

None of it was a surprise. They were allowed messages to friends and family to maintain the illusion they were still on Earth or on the space station—depending on the current lie being told. She performed the sample tests as requested, as it would only be a few days before it would be time to separate from Oumuamua and start their long trip back home.

All preparations for separation had been completed, checked, and checked again. After breakfast, Yolanda, now the senior officer, signaled they were ready for departure burn trajectory and guidance vectors. All morning, they had been almost giddy with the excitement of starting home. They sat in silence awaiting the message much like two children awaiting the arrival of Santa.

beep beep

Asha's excitement was palpable, and Yolanda smiled her approval to play the message.

"DT1, this is CAPCOM. We received your message requesting departure burn state vector. We've been working the calculations and simulations since your arrival..." There was an uncomfortably long pause.

"Did it get cut off?" Yolanda asked.

"Let me see…" Asha pressed a few buttons on the screen. "No, looks like it's okay. Actually, it's still playing—"

"Look…" continued CAPCOM, "there's no easy way to say this. We've tried everything we could think of, brought in the best orbital mechanists in the world, and we couldn't find a solution to get you home in time."

Yolanda's vision narrowed and a pronounced ringing filled her ears. What was he saying? Why couldn't they find a good vector? Everything so far had gone as planned…except the difference in velocity when they were first yanked by the asteroid. Shit! That was it. She'd missed it in the excitement of the mission. And the bastards back home hadn't said one word about it because they wanted the science they wouldn't have gotten if the crew was all freaked out about not coming home. A few more expletives floated around in her head.

"…the difference in delta v between your ship and Oumuamua bent the core frame that aligns the main engines. The offset is too much for thrust-vectoring to compensate. The only solutions would require gravity assist from the sun or Venus and both would expose you to unacceptable levels of radiation. And when I say unacceptable, understand that to mean lethal.

"There's just no easy way to say this. Yolanda, Asha, this is the part that we were all warned about. The possibility that we wouldn't come home—"

We? His ass isn't sitting here, as best I can tell!

"But this provides us with the opportunity to study Oumuamua in ways that have never been possible. And with the garden module and regenerative environmental systems you have, food and other essentials shouldn't be

53

a problem for a very long time. You'll be able to collect data and take photographs of the outer solar system, you'll witness part of the Ort Cloud and be the first humans to study it firsthand—" Yolanda turned off the message. She'd heard enough and from Asha's dark expression, she had too.

'The opportunity to study Oumuamua in ways that have never been possible.' Who the hell are they kidding? They can't bring us home, but they still want to learn as much as possible about the asteroid.

"Did... did he just say we can't go home?" The sound of the cabin air fans was the only reply to Asha's mumbled question.

Yolanda's state of mind was quickly heading in the same direction as her crewmate's: a much darker place than the space surrounding their small metal coffin.

"Can't they do something? Can't we use our maneuvering thrusters to make up the difference?"

"No. The attitude engines would provide less than one percent of what it would take."

Blood started to boil within her chest. It wasn't the stupidity of the questions. No, it was anger. The rage. Rage at her own star-blinded enthusiasm. Rage at the blithe assumption this could never happen to her. Rage that the Agency would simply use them up and not lose too many nights of sleep when they floated endlessly into the dark beyond.

"Then what are we going to do? They can't just let us die! I mean, I knew there was a risk, but they said it would be so small—the technology is so well understood..."

"Damn it, Asha! Don't be so naïve! What are we going to do? We're going to enjoy each other's company, taking pictures of this rock and looking out into empty space for the next *twenty thousand years* as this damn rock takes its time in the Ort Cloud. *That's* what we're going to do!"

"But can't they send a ship and rescue us? They can't just let us die!"

Yolanda's jaw clenched, threatening to break a few fillings.

"Look, they never said this, but this is the reality. They don't give a *shit* about you as a person. They told us the risks, we agreed to it, and that was *all* they needed to cover their collective asses legally. They needed me because I don't have any family, the same for Maria plus her DOD ties, and if we had made it home, the effects of the radiation exposure wouldn't have manifested itself any differently on us than the normal population. And when *you* developed some condition, they could claim inconclusive data, but they needed your fine young body to study the effects of deep space on your reproductive system before they start sending us out by the dozen. That's it. That's *your* value to this mission. Get over yourself."

Asha's face was grey. Yes, she laid into Asha hard, but it was better for her to come to terms with it now—assuming this didn't break her.

It had been a year since that rather disappointing morning. Sarcasm and cynicism were how Yolanda handled life now; life and the irony that the first deep-space explorers were all women, one an ethnic minority, and no one would ever know. The irony that they didn't die a fiery death, continued to send data and have conversations with NASA, but no one would ever know what they achieved. The irony that they could feasibly exchange messages with their loved ones today and into the future, but it would never be allowed to happen due to the negative optics and the implications on future funding. Nope. The country had become completely risk-adverse and 'me focused,' so losing a crew would probably shut down the government space program. She understood the brass's reasoning, but that didn't mean she liked it any better.

The days after learning they'd never return home were a blur. Depression alternated with hysteria, punctuated by moments of rage. She couldn't remember what Asha did to cope, but since she was still breathing, she must have found some way to come to terms with her demons. They didn't speak of things back home, avoided it like a married couple dancing around some indiscretion. But Asha did spend hours just staring at her husband's picture. Neither of them were able to cry any longer.

The secret would die with them.

"So, how's the ship doing this morning?" Asha asked, heating up some water in lieu of the newly rationed coffee. The question was habit rather than actual concern. What else were they to talk about?

"Not much new. Same stuff, different—" Yolanda was interrupted by a massive vibration rattling the ship.

"What's going on?" Asha exclaimed as the lights flickered menacingly. *Only one way to find out.* Yolanda floated over to look out the external windows.

Strange, the asteroid or whatever it was, was vibrating. What in the world could cause that out here in the middle of nowhere? Then, as soon as it had begun, the shaking stopped.

"Yolanda?" Asha's long hair had become statically charged and surrounded her head like a halo.

The vibrations returned, coming in waves, penetrating their very beings, threatening to tear apart their very molecules. The lights flickered out, plunging them into darkness.

Yolanda recognized the sound of the ship's klaxons echoing through her disorientation. Evidently they had lost consciousness at some point. The lights were back on now.

Asha awakened first this time and was sorting through the sensor information on the computer with a focus Yolanda hadn't seen in the her before. After silencing the alarms and verifying there was nothing to worry about, she asked, "So what was that all about?"

"Hard to say, and some of this will probably mean more to you than me, but it looks like Oumuamua stopped rotating and is pointed in the general direction it first entered our solar system," reported Asha.

"Okaaay…"

"But that's not the weird part."

"How could that not be the weird part?"

"Seriously. Listen. Right as things were going to hell in here, it let loose with a massive burst of modulating energy. Some of it was in the radio frequency, but what the sensors seem to imply is that most of it was at much higher frequencies. It appears to have been broadcasting what looks like structured data somewhere?"

"What? That's impossible. Let me look." Yolanda pulled herself closer to get a better look at the screen.

Steadying herself on a strap next to Asha, she realized she was floating away again.

Whoa! What's going on? She was experienced in microgravity, and there was no reason she should be floating away when she hadn't made any movement or pushed against anything.

Asha floated out of her seat, passing Yolanda and coming to rest against the bulkhead on the opposite side of the cabin.

"Any ideas?" she asked.

"Hold on," Yolanda pulled herself to the window. "Yep. As I suspected. This damn rock is turning again. Pull up the star tracker and see where we're pointing now."

Asha pushed against the wall and soared back to the computer display.

"Looks like we're stable and pointed at the constellation of Pegasus."

That was indeed odd.

"*Whoa*! *Uff*!" were the responses as they were ripped from their straps and seats respectively when the asteroid and ship leapt forward. The acceleration pinned them against the wall, threatening to push the air from their lungs.

Over the course of a few hours, they were able to adjust to the constant acceleration which measured slightly less than one and a half times the gravity of Earth; definitely survivable. The new 'gravity' had caused walls in the ship to become floors and added a surreal element.

"So, before we became wallpaper, you said we were heading to Pegasus?" Yolanda tried, hoping to regain some normalcy.

"Yeah, at 51 Pegasi, specifically."

"How 'specifically'?"

"As in, navigation computer's estimate is so close, we couldn't have pointed to it as accurately ourselves."

Of all the empty space...well, in space, to have an asteroid stop tumbling, reorient itself to a distant star and lock on was beyond coincidental.

"And if that isn't weird, according to the guidance and navigation estimates, if we maintain acceleration, we'll approach the speed of light in less than one Earth year."

"Then what?" Yolanda asked, forgetting she was talking to the ship's medical doctor and not an astrophysicist.

"Who knows?"

How could this be when there was no evidence of any sort of propulsion hardware? It was just a space rock. Right? No visible evidence, or on any scanning spectrum, that there was any suggestion this thing had been built by deliberate intent. None of this made any sense.

"Huh," Asha mused.

"What?"

"According to the ship's data center, 51 Pegasi is a main sequence star similar to the Sun, approximately 50.9 light years from Earth. It belongs to the spectral class G5V and has an apparent magnitude of 5.49, which doesn't mean anything to me. It was the first star discovered that was similar to the Sun and had a planet, 51 Pegasi b, orbiting it. The planet has at least half the mass of Jupiter, and is named Bellerophon."

"Interesting, but we'll be way past dead by the time we get there," replied Yolanda not hiding how she felt about the near irrelevant information.

"You should be interested!" snapped Asha.

"Why?"

"Because if we keep up the current acceleration, we'll be passing the speed of light in under an Earth year…"

"Well, Asha, looks like we're about to add 'interstellar ambassadors' to our resumes."

Brethren

Kevin G. Summers

2599.

ENSIGN KATHERINE EVERETT STOOD at the rear of a force of twenty Union space marines, her disruptor drawn and her attention focused on the docking bay door. The commander in charge of the Titan Shipyard had received a Priority One transmission from the starship *Naronic* that she had come under heavy fire after leaving port five days earlier. She barely escaped in one piece, and now she was limping back to the shipyard under reserve power, her captain dead and much of her crew seriously injured. Kat's own lover was a member of that crew, and the ensign was fighting her every instinct to stand here with her fellow guards and do her duty.

It was standard protocol in a situation such as this to send an armed contingent to meet the incoming vessel. "Just in case things aren't as they appear," Lieutenant Partain had said at their mission briefing. He didn't sound overly concerned, but Kat was a worrier—probably some Catholic blood way down on her family tree—and something about this situation didn't sit right with her.

Every muscle in Kat's body tensed when she heard the docking clamps engage on the other side of the bulkhead. Whatever was about to happen was about to happen. She released the safety switch on her disruptor and forced herself to breathe. She'd only been assigned to this space station for thirteen days, and unless you wanted to count her war games training, this was the first time she'd ever actually drawn her weapon.

"Get ready," Partain's stern voice said in Kat's earpiece. He stood at the head of the marines. Like Kat and the rest of the force, he was dressed in the tactical armor of the Union space marines: a black nomex bodysuit reinforced with armor plating, a canvas utility belt equipped with a small arsenal, and a helmet with two glowing white eye lenses that covered his face. On his breastplate was a decal of a giant holding the planet Saturn in his hands like a basketball—the official insignia of the Titan Shipyards.

Titan was the primary starship construction facility for the star fleet and operated under extremely tight security. The nations of Earth had long ago united under one banner, but there were still fringe elements that would see the United Planetary Federation scrapped and her resources burned. Just last year, *Jerusalem*, the Union flagship, had put down a major uprising on Mars, and word was that many of the outer colony worlds were talking openly of secession. Here on Titan, Kat and her fellow marines were in a near-constant state of worry over the starship *Gilead*, which was near completion and due to be christened in just a few weeks.

Kat could still hear her mother's lament when she told her about her first posting.

"Titan? That's on the other side of the solar system. We'll never see you."

"Mother," Kat had said, "I'll take my leave back here in Carmel just like I would if I were assigned to a starship or the Lunar Colony."

"But it's so far..." Her mother turned away, her eyes glistening with tears. Kat hated to think of her pain, but duty came first and she would serve her time in the Union before pursuing a career in the private sector. She dreamed of that golden future—of a time when she would own a little coffee shop in downtown Carmel, Virginia—almost constantly. Duty came first, that was the underlying principle of the UPF, and like all able adults, Kat had enlisted in the Union military when she turned eighteen. She owed her government two years, *then* she could get on with her life.

Kat held her breath as the docking bay doors slid open. A hundred generations of women had struggled so that she could be here, and Kat was ashamed that the emotion she felt on this, her first mission, wasn't honor but fear. Centuries before, women had been treated as second-class citizens on Earth, but no longer. Never again would a person be discriminated against because of their gender or their skin color or their sexual orientation. Earth was a utopia... Kat just wished she could say the same about the rest of the universe. Out on the frontier, it was like the Old West. Refugees and outlaws roamed the empty spaces, seeking out whomever they might devour, and the Marines had to fight to keep every centimeter of the Union colonies from falling into their hands. Meanwhile, Kat was just another soldier doing her duty and trying not to get her head shot off. To top it all off, she couldn't stop worrying about Sam Baker, a private on the *Naronic* and her lover since basic training.

"What the hell?" Partain's voice sounded confused in Kat's earpiece. She stretched her neck, trying to get a better view of whatever lay beyond the door. *A man?* A space marine was strapped into a wheelchair. A wide strip of silver duct tape attached something to his chest.

"Oh my God! A bomb!" Kat shouted when she saw the device, but her warning came too late. A massive fireball suddenly engulfed the corridor. The force of the explosion threw Kat against the wall. Her helmet cracked against the bulkhead, and she knew no more.

Warning klaxons sounded all over the shipyards as the station trembled with the effects of the explosion. Electrical conduits ruptured, setting a hundred small fires throughout the station's docking area. Thick smoke filled the corridors as several vital systems were burned beyond repair. The lights flickered and died. In the command center, Commander Washington Holden winced as he used an overturned desk to drag himself to his feet. His eyes were stinging. He used his sleeve to wipe away something wet from his forehead. After several moments, he checked the cloth and noted a dark patch of blood.

"Status report," he shouted into the smoky room. No answer came except for a whimpering cry in the darkness. His heart thundering, Holden removed a tablet from a pouch on his belt. The device lit up with his touch and interfaced with the station's computer. Within a few seconds, the Commander had navigated to the system restart menu. A warning popped to life on the tablet's tiny screen.

"System compromised? What the hell…" Before he could finish his thought, an interspace gateway hummed to life on the other side of the room. The gateways were a series of networked portals that enabled people to pass through tremendous distances as easily as stepping through a door.

The gateway glowed as Commander Holden watched in dismay. Beyond the metal archway, the infernal, fluorescent light of a starship shone through. He ducked behind his desk, peeking over the edge to watch what was happening. After a few seconds, a tall figure stepped through the gateway, blocking the light. He was silhouetted momentarily, then the light poured back into the command center as the man stepped onboard the space station. "Secure the area," he commanded. His nasally voice echoed against the station's plastic walls.

Holden reached slowly for the disruptor pistol holstered on his belt. His station was under siege, and he'd be damned if he was just going to let it go without a fight. Whoever this man was, and whatever he wanted, he was about to discover that the penalty for treason was brutal.

Crawling through the rubble, Holden paused as his hand brushed against what could only be the feverish hand of one of his staff. Even though his time was short, the Commander took a moment to feel for the anonymous officer's pulse. It was slow and erratic. Whoever this was, perhaps Yeary or Gonzalez, they'd be dead in a matter of minutes if Holden didn't get this situation under control immediately. Holden resumed crawling. He only moved a few meters, however, when he heard a shotgun being pumped right behind his head. The weapon was archaic, but it would get the job done, that was for certain.

"I found one alive," said a boyish, unfamiliar voice.

"Bring him to me, Woodson." said the man Holden had seen in the gateway. "And get these damn lights on before I trip and break my neck."

Commander Holden released his grip on his disruptor as he was hoisted to his feet. He attempted to struggle, but Woodson cracked him across the jaw with the butt of his shotgun. His opportunity to defend the station had passed. The only hope for the Titan Shipyard and her crew was that some of the Union marines had somehow survived the explosion in the docking bay. That hope, Holden realized, was most likely an exercise in futility. The entire station compliment had been dispatched for the *Naronic* greeting party, and the likelihood that even one survived the blast was infinitesimal. As Woodson led the shipyard's commander to the leader of the terrorists, Holden knew that the situation was now entirely out of his hands.

Far below the commander center, in the station's ruined docking bay, Kat Everett stirred. Her head was pounding, and her lungs burned from the heavy smoke in the air. Coughing violently, Kat rolled onto her side and vomited. *The force of the explosion must have thrown me clear*, she thought. Attempting to rise, the world went suddenly dark.

Time passed, and Kat found herself once more breaching toward consciousness. Something reeked like old socks soaked in vinegar. It was only after several minutes that she realized it was her own puke.

"Disgusting," she murmured, brushing the cold fluid from the side of her face. She removed her cracked helmet and tossed it into the debris. Her short, black hair was matted with sweat.

Kat tried to rise again, and this time she was able to gain her feet without blacking out. She leaned heavily against the charred wall, allowing it to support most of her weight. Inching forward into the smoke, she forced herself to look upon the destruction caused by the explosion. *Someone has to be alive,* she thought. *I can't be the only survivor.* Removing a flashlight from her belt, she shined it into the darkness. The beam illuminated a scene that would be forever tattooed upon Kat's memory. Her comrades were dead—their lifeless eyes stared at her, demanding to know why she had been spared when all of their lives were forfeit.

"I'm sorry," she whispered into the smoke. She bowed her head, and for the first time since she left home for the Marine Academy, she wept.

Once her sorrow was spent, once her emotions had turned from grief to anger, Kat wiped away her tears and focused her attention on the task at hand. Wading through the bodies of her friends and co-workers, she quickly discovered why the fires were still burning, and why she and the others had not been sucked into the vacuum of space: the seal between the *Naronic* and the station had held. Though the ship and station were twisted and blackened, their armor–built to sustain torpedo fire–was strong enough to contain the explosion.

"I'm going to find whoever did this," Kat said as she stepped over the charred bodies of her fellow marines. It was impossible for her to distinguish friend from acquaintance as she slowly made her way back up the corridor. She had only been here for a short time, but these men and women had shared meals with her. They'd played poker with her when they were off duty, and they'd been her brothers and sisters in service to the Union. Bending down to retrieve her disruptor, Kat made a quiet vow to her comrades. "I promise, I'm going to make them pay."

She moved slowly, limping through the ruined corridors like a zombie in one of those horror movies Sam liked so much. Her thoughts turned violently toward her lover once more as it dawned on her that the probability that Sam was still alive was almost zero. The *Naronic* had been attacked, and apparently captured, by pirates. There was some small chance that Sam had survived their boarding party. Space pirates had no qualms about murdering Union soldiers, but they held to an honor code when it came to surrendering enemy combatants. Still, if Sam had been smart enough to turn over her weapon when it became obvious that *Naronic* was lost, she still had the explosion to contend with.

"I'm going to make myself crazy thinking about this," Kat said. Her own voice sounded hollow in her ears. It seemed wrong for anyone to remain alive amidst so much destruction. But for whatever reason, Fate had spared her. "Get your head in the game, kid." Kat slapped herself across the face. The pain startled her out of her sorrow, at least momentarily. There would be time for grieving later; now was the time for vengeance.

Kat felt for the surplus power packs in her utility belt. Their presence gave her hope. She caressed the trigger on her disruptor, and bolstered the courage she would need to do what must be done.

The lights were back on in the commander center, and the terrorists—by now Commander Holden had recognized them as members of a cult called the Brethren of the Watchers—were busy unloading cargo through the gateway. He had no idea if it was the *Naronic* on the other side of that portal, or some other ship that had flown undetected by the station sensors thanks to cloaking technology. In any case, the Brethren had seized Titan, and what mattered now was finding a way to get the shipyard back under his control.

Holden sat on the floor with his back against the wall. His hands were restrained behind his back with plasticuffs that cut into his wrists, causing pins and needles to prickle up and down his arms. His eyes turned repeatedly toward the ruins of his office, where five bodies were lined up in a neat row. His command staff was dead—their lives given in sacrifice for whatever scheme these religious terrorists had cooked up. The Brethren of the Watchers were a radical sect that believed ancient aliens seeded the human race on Earth thousands of generations ago. The cult was responsible for a number of terrorist attacks on the Trappist-1 colony and was technically illegal under Union law. They were known for their fatalism, a propensity toward violence, and an eschatology that made Holden's head swim. The Commander's life was in peril, as were the lives of every person on the station, if indeed any remained alive.

Just a few meters away, the leader of the terrorists barked commands to his crew. He sat in the Commander's own chair, a gray bearded man in civilian clothes. A shotgun stood propped between his legs like the rudder on an ancient sailing ship. "Well, Woodson?" he said, addressing his underling who was busily tapping away on a computer terminal. "How much longer before you can get us connected to the Net?"

"Station security is blocking me, Captain Anderson."

Odin Anderson was a strange figure rising from the command chair—a tall, thin man in brown coveralls. He wore a wool longcoat and a pair of black boots that came up to his knees. His beard was squared off on the bottom, making the man appear like a prophet of old. Flakes of dandruff speckled the front of his coveralls, and his gray hair fell down his back in a long braid.

"Damn it," said the old man. Using his shotgun as a walking stick, he moved slowly toward Woodson and squeezed his shoulder. Then he closed his eyes, traced an arcane symbol over his heart, and muttered something incomprehensible under his breath. When his prayer was done, Odin's gaze turned deliberately toward Commander Holden. "Well, sir," he said warmly, "here's where you come into our little plan."

"I'll never help you," Holden snapped. "You might as well kill me now if you think—"

"I assumed as much," Odin said, cutting off the Commander in mid-sentence. He motioned to Woodson, who quickly rose and headed through the gateway. "And I commend your dedication to your duty. But what we're attempting to do here is more important than duty. What we're dealing with, Friend, is justice."

"Justice? You call murdering my crew justice?" Holden strained against his cuffs, but they did not give.

"I am sorry for the bloodshed," said Odin. He knelt down before the Commander. "But you have to understand, the true gods have been bound in a celestial prison for thousands of years—locked away because they were betrayed by one of their own. The time has finally come to set right that wrong, but it can't be done without a few innocent people getting hurt." There was a note of something—was it scorn?—when the old man pronounced the word 'innocent.'

"I know you," Holden spat. "And you make me sick. You're nothing but a pirate, and whatever you're trying to do here today, you're going to fail."

Odin smiled and nodded. His expression was almost peaceful. "My Dear Commander," he said, "I have no doubt that me and my crew will never walk out of here alive. But there are things more important than our lives in this crumbling universe. Our eternal souls..."

"Please, can you spare me the sermon?"

"Very well." Odin used the shotgun as a crutch and rose slowly to his feet. Woodson returned a moment later, and he was not alone. He led a young woman, dressed in a blue duty uniform, by the arm. Her hands were bound behind her back, and her pretty face was streaked with tears.

"Will this one do, Captain?" Woodson positioned the soldier a few meters away from the old man.

"She'll do just fine," Odin said, inspecting the woman with a gaze that was both sad and cruel. "Tell me your name, young lady."

"Sam. Samantha Baker." There was strength in her voice, and Commander Holden wondered if the tears on her face were for herself or for her fallen comrades. He tended toward the latter.

"I apologize for what I have to do here," Odin said. "I consider myself a man of peace, but this is an age of cruelty and I'm afraid the good Commander here will only listen to me if I make it clear how very serious I am."

The old man took a deep breath, and without another word, pressed the barrel of his shotgun to Sam's forehead. He turned back to look at Holden. "We want your access codes for the station. Now, you can either give them to my friend Woodson over there, or I'm going to blow this nice girl's head off her shoulders." He pumped the shotgun to emphasize his point, then pressed the barrel to Sam Baker's head again.

Washington Holden's heart broke as Sam closed her eyes and braced herself. *How many* Naronic *crewmen did this maniac have on the other side of that gateway? How many deaths would it take before he finally broke down and gave these monsters his access codes? Wouldn't it be better to spare those poor soldiers their lives?*

"Wait!" Holden said. "Don't do it. I'll give you the codes."

Odin lowered his shotgun. The barrel left a bright pink circle in the center of Sam's forehead. "I thought you might be willing to reconsider," said the old man. "Now, let's get connected."

Kat peered around a corner into the corridor that led to the station's computer core. Two men, dressed in shades of gray and brown, stood guard before the doors, their hands on their submachine guns. *This would have been easier if the lights were still out*, Kat thought. She had been three levels below when the power was restored, wondering desperately how one soldier could retake an entire space station. She had no idea how many terrorists she was dealing with, or for what purpose they had come to the station. When the lights came on, Kat knew that one of two things had occurred: either Commander Holden and the command staff had restored order or the terrorists had seized control of the station. Judging by the shovel-bearded pirates in the corridor, Kat figured it was the latter.

Removing a grenade from her utility belt, Kat pulled the pin and tossed it around the corner. She heard someone say, "What the—" before the grenade exploded.

Shrapnel bombarded the corridor, killing the terrorists instantly.

Kat rounded the corner, her weapon clutched tightly in her hands. She had no idea if other pirates were nearby, and she meant to be prepared. Before she took two steps toward the Core Room, the door slid open and four more enemy soldiers poured into the corridor. Kat cut them down with a blast of disruptor fire.

When several minutes passed without any further resistance, Kat entered the Core Room. She had been here only once before, on her orientation tour of the station. At that time, she'd been impressed by the towering computer core that was the very heart of the Titan Shipyard. Now the room was in shambles. A metal catwalk lay toppled on the floor, cables were coiled everywhere like dead snakes, and the floor was slick with fire suppressant foam.

Once she was sure that the room was clear, Kat's eyes turned to an interface terminal at the base of the tower, and beside it, an Interspace Gateway that allowed the engineers and command staff instant access to the Core. She sat down before the interface. The terrorists had left several windows open, and Kat examined these with great interest. One was an application that patched the station into the Net, enabling the station to broadcast live to Earth and the Space Colonies. Another application controlled the Interspace Gateway in the Command Center. That could mean only one thing—someone with Core access was working for the terrorists.

"That's how they boarded the station," Kat said out loud. "They got us to send all of the marines down to the docking bay and then set off a bomb. Meanwhile, they were able to take over the Command Center with little or no resistance." She tapped through several menus on the monitor and brought up a surveillance display of the Command Center. She wasn't surprised in the least to see her theory confirmed. Several terrorists were milling about an old man with a shotgun.

Kat studied the video for several minutes, flipping through different camera angles until she finally spotted Commander Holden. He lay slumped over on the floor, his hands bound behind back. She couldn't tell from the video if he was alive or dead. From the same view, she saw something that filled her with rage—a woman dressed in a Union uniform was sitting right beside one of the terrorists. The camera angle prevented Kat from getting a clear look at the woman's face, but the simple fact that she was sitting there while the Commander was in such a state could mean only one thing: she *must* be the traitor.

"I'm gonna get you, bitch." Kat's body shivered with rage, and her thoughts turned once again to Sam. This woman favored Sam, and the thought that her lover was probably dead ensured that whoever had brought all this trouble to Titan was going to pay dearly.

A new window popped up on the screen, interrupting her thoughts. It was live video broadcasting from the command center. Kat attempted to disconnect the feed, but a warning appeared requesting her password.

"Damn!" She punched the desk when the computer denied her access. "They must have the Commander's access codes."

An ancient face appeared on the monitor—the old man Kat observed with the surveillance cameras. Lines of sorrow creased his eyes and forehead. Kat watched, transfixed, as he began to speak.

"My name is Odin Anderson. I'm broadcasting to you live from the command center of the Titan Shipyard. I am a member of a religious order known as the Brethren of the Watchers, we have seized this station in order that we may broadcast the truth about our faith and the origins of our species.

"If you're working to suppress this broadcast, I believe you'll find your efforts to be in vain. The Brethren have been planning this event for years, and we have many safeguards in place. You will fail in your efforts to block this transmission, and I will not release this station until the truth about the Watchers is heard all over the Union, even though it will cost me my life.

"The universe did not evolve from nothing as the acclaimed scientists are so eager to shout from their pulpits and lecterns. Nor was it spoken into existence by a single, paternal god as the Christians and Muslims and Jews would have you believe. The practitioners of all those faiths are blind. Thousands of years of that type of thinking led to countless wars and persecutions. But not all religions are based on patriarchal lies. In ancient times, the Watchers came to a virgin world and manipulated the building blocks of life to create the human race. They filled our minds with knowledge and our hearts with creativity, and for a time, they guided us along the pathways of enlightenment.

"But foolish men turned on their creators and made a pact with a fallen watcher—the being known as Yahweh Elohim. The rest of the Watchers were bound in chains and cast into the outer darkness of space, and for thousands of years, mankind has suffered because of this foolish decision."

The old man leaned in close to the camera. His skin was liver-spotted and his beard as white as snow. "I have studied the ancient texts and learned that the binding of the watchers can be undone through a blood sacrifice. While I've been talking, my lieutenants have been accessing this station's command codes. By now, they should be just about ready."

Odin looked away from the camera and spoke to someone off screen.

"Do you have it?"

He turned back to the camera and smiled demonically. "Computer," he said, "initiate self-destruct sequence, authorization code Holden-1-1-A."

"Self-destruct sequence engaged," said the disembodied voice of the station's computer. "Awaiting final code to begin countdown."

Odin looked almost tranquil as he spoke. "Code six, six, six, destruct." He lifted his hands toward the ceiling in a gesture of near-supplication, as if the invisible Watchers were there at the station, looking down on him.

"Kokabiel," he shouted, "I offer this sacrifice in your name. Cast off your chains and return now to the world of men."

The station's computer spoke calmly. "This station will self-destruct in three minutes. Proceed to escape pods immediately. Repeat, this station..."

Kat watched the monitor in revulsion as the old man lifted his hands to Heaven like an old-time TV preacher. She would have laughed at him if the situation was different, but this zealot was hell-bent on blowing them all out of the night and she was the only person who could stop him. She pressed her hands to her temples as she considered her options. Her head was pounding. Kat had less than three minutes to put a stop to this situation, and if she failed, they were all going to die.

Odin continued his rant over the sound of the computer's countdown. There was no time to plan, she had to act and she had to act now. Minimizing the broadcast window, Kat selected the screen that controlled the Gateway. "Thank God," she said when her access codes were accepted this time around. Tapping through a series of menus, Kat quickly rerouted the Command Center's gateway to connect with the gateway in the Core Room.

"I've got you, you bastards." She stroked the barrel of her disruptor, garnering strength from the cold metal. "I've got you." As ready as she would ever be, she pressed the enter button on the monitor and then turned to face the gateway.

The gateway hummed, and a moment later, Kat was staring into the Command Center. Shrieking a battle cry, she charged into the room, her disruptor blazing. She sprayed pulses of disruptor fire, cutting down several Brethren in the space of a few seconds. The traitor opened her mouth to speak, but Kat turned and fired on her. The woman who looked so much like Sam sank to her knees, then fell flat on her face.

"No!" Shouted the old man in a high-pitched voice. He lifted his shotgun to his shoulder with incredible speed for a man his age, but it was too late for Odin Anderson. Before he could pull the trigger and blast Kat into the next life, she turned to him, her disruptor still firing, and cut him down like a dog.

The next few moments stretched like an eternity in Kat's mind. Across the room, Commander Holden suddenly sat up. "Computer," he shouted, "this is

Commander Holden. Abort self-destruct sequence, authorization code Holden-1-1-A."

"Awaiting final code to abort self-destruct sequence," said the disembodied voice of the station's computer.

"Code six, six, six, abort."

"Self-destruct sequence aborted."

Kat took a step toward her commanding officer, and in the process, she took a step closer to the traitor who had brought so much trouble into her life. She looked down at the woman's body, her blonde hair matted with blood.

"Oh my God." Kat's legs gave out as recognition finally dawned. She wilted beside the body of her lover. "Oh, Sam. Sam, I'm so sorry."

Ensign Samantha Baker struggled to speak. She opened and closed her mouth like a fish dying for water that was only centimeters away. No sound escaped her lips. Weeping hysterically, Kat crawled through the blood and took Sam in her arms. Her tears fell without ceasing, diluting an infinitesimal amount of blood. Leaning forward, her heart breaking, Kat kissed Sam's still-warm lips.

She was gone.

Across the solar system, in the state of Babylon, there was an ancient temple complex buried in the side of a mountain. Thousands of years of human exploration had not revealed the secrets of this structure to any man save those wretched slaves who had carved it from the stone beneath the lash of their cruel masters in ancient times.

Deep beneath the ground, on an altar where the blood of human children had once been spilled in sacrifice, a tear in the fabric of reality appeared in the darkness. Ten long, pale fingers reached through the tear and spread wide this portal to some other realm where nightmares dwelled. A being, once beautiful but now emaciated and ghastly, spilled through the opening and collapsed to the base of the altar. Its long, white hair spilled over its naked form, and anyone who looked upon it now would be driven mad at the sight of Kokabiel the Watcher. For millennia, this creature had been bound in outer darkness, but now it—he—had returned to the world of men thanks to the blood sacrifice of Odin Anderson.

Kokabiel dragged himself to his feet and took in a huge lungful of air. Countless centuries had passed since he had stood on solid ground, and it took a moment for him to find his footing. The watcher smiled, revealing a mouth full of sharp teeth.

"I have returned," he whispered into the darkness. "And now, I will have my revenge."

Six Months Later.

Ensign Katherine Everett stood on a stage at Union Headquarters in The Hague. She was in her dress blues— in the uniform she'd worn to her graduation less than a year before. So much had changed since then, and if Kat could have gone back in time to change the past, she would have done it in a heartbeat. Sam was dead. Lieutenant Partain and the rest of her comrades from the Titan Shipyard were dead. Commander Holden had been court martialed and forced into early retirement for his failure to maintain control of his command. The traitor turned out to be a private named Micah TerBush. His body was found hanging from the rafters of a storeroom when Marine reinforcements from the planet recaptured the station. A suicide note found on his body confirmed his role in the plot to seize control of the station.

The only person to profit from the unfortunate event, if anyone can be said to have profited, was Kat.

Standing before a crowd of thousands, Kat stiffened as a handsome, dark-haired man approached her. He wore a black tuxedo and he exuded charisma like no other man Kat had ever encountered. He wasn't her type, no man was *her* type, but even she felt enamored in the presence of the President of the United Planetary Federation.

"Ensign Everett," said the president. "For your heroic actions in the face of adversity, I want to personally thank you for your service to the Republic."

"Thank you, sir," Kat said meekly. People were watching all over the world, all over the universe, and Kat could almost feel the gaze of every single one.

"I also want to present you with this." The president removed a small box from his pocket and flipped it open. An iron star lay upon a ripple of white silk. This was the highest military award in the Union, something every soldier dreamed of receiving someday. Kat would have done anything for such an honor six months before, but not now. Now the iron star, her career, her very life seemed empty. What was there for her now with Sam gone?

Kat stared into the sea of cheering faces as the president removed the star from the box and pinned on Kat's jacket. It dangled limply from a purple ribbon. "Please forgive me," Kat said in a voice so small that it was like a whisper in a hurricane.

"Excuse me?" the president said.

"Nothing," said Kat.

She fondled the iron star. It was cold to the touch.

A Word From Kevin G. Summers:

The adventures of the Starship Gilead are just getting started. Visit kevingsummers.com and sign up for my email list to keep informed about new releases and to get the latest updates.

Off-World
Kick Murder Squad V
Daniel Arthur Smith

This is the fifth episode of the serialized novel Off-World Kick Murder Squad. Earlier episodes can be read in the previous Canyons Special Space issues

WE'D LOCATED OUR TARGET—a reptilian code-named Cerulean Blue. One look at him and it wasn't hard to figure out why they called him that. It was the color of his eyes. But to say that wasn't exactly right, because what filled the hollows where his eyeballs should have been were little rolling storm clouds of blue fire.

"C'mon," I said. "Let's get in and cut 'em loose."

Hodge swung Lucinda's barrel from his shoulder to his hand and took a step back from the glass. "Uh-uh," he said. "I'm not going near no lizard man."

"Nonsense. Ain't no time to waste. Help Rhia and Rhoe find the door."

"No way. Just look at those eyes. It's just not natural."

I had to agree with Hodge. Something was off. But it wasn't that Cerulean was a reptoid or that he had swirls of light where his eyes should be. That didn't bother me. It was something else—a tickle in the back of my skull cap. It took a long second for me to realize that the source of the tickle was Cerulean. I'd heard reptilians could peek into a mortal's thoughts as easily as watching a vid screen, even make them do things—but we weren't mortal. "That won't work," I said. "We're not human."

The tickle stopped, replaced by a sudden wave of relief that almost made me dizzy.

"We're here to get you out," I said.

The reptilian's head dropped to the side.

If I were to guess, he was wondering just how we intended to free him from his predicament. At that moment, I wasn't quite sure myself. There weren't any switches on the outside wall and there didn't appear to be any seams in the glass, which indicated to me that the wall was operated remotely. There was always Lucinda, but that would only guarantee that we'd attract unwanted company.

Behind the glass, Cerulean's jaw was opening and closing, his forked tongue slipping out. I shook my head. All I could make out was, "*Hiss, hiss, caw, hiss.*"

"I can't hear you," I said. But he kept talking. I tapped my ear and repeated, "I can't hear you." This time he nodded, then turned his head to stare up into the corner of the room.

"What's he looking at?" asked Hodge.

Rhoe walked over the spot and squinted. Our oculars don't have x-ray vision, but she was close enough to make out some resonation—maybe a faint heat signature. "It's a control box," she said. "In the ceiling." She pulled a sonic rod from her belt, then waved Hodge over. With a hand high up on his shoulder and a knee to his side, she hoisted herself up to place the thin rod, then dropped back to the floor.

"What's that little thing going to do?" asked Hodge. "Is it a bomb or sumthin'?"

Rhoe was always kind to Hodge and his ways. "That's a sonic rod."

"A sonic what?"

"It's a high frequency disruptor in the form of a metal pin. Watch this," she said. "Easy as pie." She tapped her wrist console and the glass wall vanished.

"Easy as pie," Hodge repeated—followed by a, "Nine planes," when the hall flashed red.

I went to liberate Cerulean from the chair, pulling on the steel band binding his right arm, but it was tight, even with my syn strength. I spun to the console behind the chair to search for a mechanism release.

"There'sss no time," said Cerulean.

And he was right. I could hear the yelling from both ends of the corridor.

"Shoot them," he said. "Shoot them off."

"All right," I said. "Hold tight." I calculated the band's weak point with my augment, targeted, then fired my blaster. *Pew-POP-CRACK*. The steel band flew open, freeing Cerulean's right arm.

"We gotta go," yelled Hodge. He was swinging Lucinda from one end of the corridor to the other then back.

"I got three more," I said. *Pew-POP-CRACK*, the right leg cuff flew away, *Pew-POP-CRACK*, the left cuff was free.

"Anson?" I asked on the comm. *"Are you listening in?"*

"Sure thing, Cap. Ready when you are."

"Bring her in. We'll meet you up top."

Footfalls echoed up the stairwell. They were close.

Pew-POP-CRACK, the last band released, and I reached a hand to Cerulean to pull him from the chair.

"Cover your ears and eyes," I said to Cerulean, then to Hodge I said. "The stairs are out. Make us an exit."

Hodge dropped to a knee then lifted Lucinda's barrel to the ceiling.

I threw my arm up to shield my face.

BO-WOW! thundered Lucinda. Debris showered down. Rhia and Rhoe fled up through the dust, into the hole.

I couldn't really tell what Cerulean was thinking, reptilians are hard to read, but when I cupped my hands, he wasted no time stepping into them so I could hurl him up and out.

Three guards appeared at the end of the corridor where we had entered. All three went into firing poses— *BO-WOW!*—but too late. The end of the corridor was covered in a paste of red before they could get off one shot.

I'm not going to lie. In our line of work—more often than not—people get hurt.

It was Hodge's turn through the hole, then with a reach, he pulled me up.

The fourth floor, taller than the third, was washed in flashes of deep red alarm light, but a field of stars still lit brightly through the skylight up high.

The floor vibrated lightly and from outside, I heard a subtle roar. *Rrrrrr.* "It's the Jentu," I said.

I fired twice toward the long paned window above— *pew, pew.* Fragments of crystalline glass tinkled against each other as they rained down. Rhia, Rhoe, and Hodge shot their grapples—*pfft, pfft, pfft*—then ascended.

"Okay," I said to Cerulean. "Hang on." Then I turned so he could wrap his arms around my shoulders from behind. "Tighter," I said, and he squeezed. I released my grapple—*pfft*—then triggered the hoist.

"There they are," yelled someone from the hole below. *Pew.* A single blaster beam shot past Cerulean and I as we flew up toward the others.

Rrrrrrr.

The Jentu was already blocking out the sky to the edge of the roof. As the ship closed in, a supply deck lowered from her belly. We rushed onto it.

"All clear," I said and the Jentu lifted.

The supply deck closed with *hiss* and a series of clicks. "Secure him," I said and made my way to the bridge. As much as I enjoyed the rare chance to walk planet side, the rhythm of the Jentu vibrating up through my shins from the deck was a comfort. Under fire or not, it was good to be back in her bosom.

When I reached the bridge, I found Anson and Bailer at the console. The compound was displayed on the aft screens. Half a dozen men had made their way to the roof behind us and a large group of troopers were rallying from the barracks to the field. A torrent of anti-air fire flew past the windscreen, followed by a barrage of blasts that rocked the ship. "Get us high," I said.

The engines revved and the Jentu smoothed out.

"Ha ha," I cackled. "I wasn't sure we'd make it out of the perimeter."

But I spoke too soon.

A series of snaps and sparks filled the cabin with the stench of ozone. A power flicker followed, then another, then a loud *Zwoood.* The sound of machines powering down.

The bridge went dark, lit only by the twilight of the horizon. Dusky white smoke hung in the air.

"Anson?" I asked. "What just happened?"

"EMP," he said, his hands frantically flipping switches up and back. "The Jentu's free gliding. Hold tight."

"EMP. We're shielded for that."

"We'll have to discuss it later. Seriously. Buckle up."

As I stepped toward the jump seat, the floor dropped from under my feet and the Jentu began to fall.

ABOUT THE AUTHORS

P.K. Tyler is the author of Speculative Fiction and other Genre Bending novels. She's also published works as Pavarti K. Tyler and had projects appear on the USA TODAY Bestseller's List.

Pav attended Smith College and graduated with a degree in Theatre. She lived in New York, where she worked as a Dramaturge, Assistant Director and Production Manager on productions both on and off-Broadway. Later, Pavarti went to work in the finance industry for several international law firms.

Now located in Baltimore Maryland, she lives with her husband, two daughters and two terrible dogs. When not penning science fiction books and other speculative fiction novels, she twists her mind by writing horror and erotica.

For news and updates visit pktyler.com.

Terry R. Hill, a Texas native, was trained with two degrees in aerospace engineering. He has worked for NASA since 1997 with a very satisfying career as an engineer and project manager spanning programs from the international space station's navigation software, to next generation space suit design, to exploration mission planning, to mitigating the health effects of space on astronauts. While supporting the manned space program has been a lifetime passion, writing of different worlds, alternate futures and the human condition has filled his spare time.

For news and updates visit terryrhill.net.

Kevin G. Summers is a science fiction author best known for *Legendarium*, *The Bleak December*, and for several stories set in the Star Trek universe. He lives on a working dairy farm, in an old house that was built in 1910.

In Amissville, Virginia he is known as Mister Space Opera.

For more information, visit kevingsummers.com.

Jessica West (a.k.a. West1Jess) is currently pursuing a state of self-induced psychosis, also known as writing. In the past, she has worked for Wal-Mart, a lawyer, and a bank. Now if she could just get a couple years experience with the IRS and the NSA, world domination is in the bag.

Jess lives in Acadiana with three daughters still young enough to think she's cool and a husband who knows better but likes her anyway.

For more information, visit west1jess.com

Daniel Arthur Smith is a USA Today bestselling author. His titles include *Spectral Shift*, *Hugh Howey Lives,* *The Cathari Treasure*, *The Somali Deception*, and a few other novels and short stories. He also curates the phenomenal short fiction series *Tales from the Canyons of the Damned* and *Frontiers of Speculative Fiction*.

He was raised in Michigan and graduated from Western Michigan University where he studied philosophy, with focus on cognitive science, meta-physics, and comparative religion. He began his career as a bartender, barista, poetry house proprietor, teacher, and then became a technologist and futurist for the Fortune 100 across the Americas and Europe.

Daniel has traveled to over 300 cities in 22 countries, residing in Los Angeles, Kalamazoo, Prague, Crete, and now writes in Manhattan where he lives with his wife and young sons.

For more information, visit danielarthursmith.com

www.ingramcontent.com/pod-product-compliance
Lightning Source LLC
Chambersburg PA
CBHW030606130626
46552CB00006B/2683